The Woman Outlaw

Legas

Sicilian Studies Series
Series Editor: Gaetano Cipolla
Volume VIII

Other volumes ublished in this series:

Maria Rosa Cutrufelli

The Woman Outlaw

(La Briganta)

Translated into English by
Angela M. Jeannet

LEGAS

Library of Congress Cataloging-in-Publication Data

Cutrufelli, Maria Rosa.
  [Briganta. English]
  The woman outlaw : (La briganta) / Maria Rosa Cutrufelli ; translated into English by Angela M. Jeannet.
      p. cm. — (Sicilian studies ; v. 8)
  ISBN 1-881901-40-8 (pbk.)
  I. Jeannet, Angela M. II. Title. III. Series.
PQ4863.U75B7513 2004
853'.914—dc22

                              2004001758

Acknowledgments
The publisher is grateful to Arba Sicula and Franklin and Marshall College for their generous grants that in part made the publication of this book possible.

The publisher also thanks Giulia Di Filippi for the use of her painting for the cover.

For information and for orders, write to:
Legas

P.O. Box 149   3 Wood Aster Bay
Mineola, New York   Ottawa, Ontario
11501, USA   KR2 1B3 Canada

legaspublishing.com

For Paula, my best reader
AMJ

Table of Contents

Introduction

Angela M. Jeannet

The twentieth century will be remembered in Italian literature as the women's century. At no time before did so many women write, publish, and enjoy public and critical acclaim. The 1900s opened with Grazia Deledda, a winner of the Nobel prize for literature, and closed on the achievements of a number of excellent fiction writers, Anna Banti, Natalia Ginzburg, and Elsa Morante among others. The writings of twentieth-century Italian women may differ in style and thematics but they have in common two characteristics: a keen interest in history, and the importance they give to gender, as it affects and subverts our definition and understanding of history. The stories they tell open a wider perspective on the universe of human passions and struggles, in a great variety of situations. Maria Rosa Cutrufelli's *The Woman Outlaw* (*La briganta*)emerges from that background and finds its place in Italian literature at a time when women's voices are already self-assured and range widely over the potential material to be used for the work of the imagination.

The novella's historical framework is provided by the events that changed Italy's fate approximately between 1860 and 1880, from the years preceding Garibaldi's arrival in Sicily to the time of the consolidation of the new Kingdom of Italy. That period is fundamental in Italian history and is the subject of studies too numerous to list exhaustively.[1] It marks the moment when the country's unification was within reach, but also when—in the view of many, and not exclusively Southerners—the greatest betrayal of the *Risorgimento* spirit was perpetrated. It is significant that the movement aiming at the attainment of Italian union and independence was called "Resurrection" (*Risorgimento*). The name, with its quasi-mystical undertones, was meant to be a reminder that Italy was destined to be one and independent because of the legacies of Roman antiquity, the traditions of its "high" culture, and a common literary language. Some of the inhabitants of the Italian peninsula—

9

North, Center, and South—had resented for centuries the direct or indirect domination by a variety of foreign powers, and evidence of that resentment is not hard to find from the 1300s on.[2] Whether such ideals were the sole province of cultured citizens of the various regions, or not, is debatable and has been debated. In fact, the social and economic conditions differed enormously in the various parts of the Italian peninsula, and the drive toward nationhood was unevenly felt by the (future) Italian populace. The *Risorgimento* was undoubtedly a minority-driven insurrection.

Because of that fact, and because of its timing, the movement was marked from the beginning, in the wake of the Napoleonic wars, by diplomatic intricacies and compromises; only the conquest of Rome in 1870 concluded the formation of the Kingdom of Italy. In other words, while the rest of Europe was facing the transformations brought about by the impact of the Industrial Revolution, and made the first moves toward colonialism, Italy was still laboriously attempting to coalesce into a modern nation. The peninsula was a mosaic of small principalities propped up by foreign forces; they had retained none of the grandeur they had in the Renaissance, and survived as archaic reminders of feudal times. The birth of a nation named Italy was a goal that many political observers believed to be unattainable. Powerful interests and conflicting visions pitted against each other several groups of participants, in a confrontation of European dimensions. On the one side were the Italian patriots—mostly moderately well-to-do landowners, or intellectuals—and the diplomats of the ruling family of the Kingdom of Piedmont and Sardinia, who saw in the insurrections an opportunity for their small state's expansion. The various European nation-states were divided on the issue because, precisely at that time, they were vying with each other for dominance on the world map. Some of them favored Italian unity in hopes of gaining a new ally, while some feared the formation of yet another national state competing for power. The State of the Vatican feared losing its domains that went well beyond the city of Rome to include much of Central Italy; and the Kingdom of the Two Sicilies, which included the entire South and the largest Mediterranean island, was already struggling against popular unrest and was fighting to avoid its own demise. By the 1860s, uprisings calling for freedom had taken place in various parts of the peninsula, and plebiscites had quickly brought together most Northern and Central Italian regions

It was then that Giuseppe Garibaldi decided to contribute to the reunion of all the regions of Italy by moving against the forces of the Kingdom of the Two Sicilies. His army, made up of little more than one thousand volunteers wearing red shirts, has become a legend. It succeeded in freeing the entire Southern part of the peninsula but was checked in its triumphal march toward Rome by the Piedmontese army. The hopes that Garibaldi's intervention in Sicily had stirred, for social justice and a more equitable distribution of the immense Sicilian estates, faded once the former Kingdom of the Two Sicilies was annexed to the Kingdom of Italy. The new government was oblivious to the plight of wretched peasants, and feared the revolts aimed at eliminating the traditional structures of Southern landowning; it continued, and—if possible—exacerbated, the policies of the rulers it replaced. Taxation, military conscription, and discrimination embittered Southern Italians. Any attempts at bringing back the former rulers, and the riots of later years, were brutally quelled by troops that were called "Italian" but were viewed by most Sicilians as foreign. The tormented history behind the official narrative of Italian unification is evidence of major differences, misunderstandings, and unending hostilities between the various social classes and regional groups of "Italians." Reappraisals and revisions of the *Risorgimento* are at the center of the national debate even today. They are the subject of scholarly essays, newspaper articles, and political debates, as Italy—after a century and a half of struggles as a united and independent entity—attempts to redefine and understand its own profoundly transformed self.

The phenomenon of brigandage was one inheritance that feudalism, once rampant in Southern Italy, bequeathed the new nation. In all likelihood it had multiple sources. Various observers and scholars have suggested different possibilities as to its origins. In the nineteenth century, some armed bands were made up of men hired by landowning families as a sort of private militia to enforce the families' rule over their estates and to harass other families. Other bands were formed by artisans and peasants who had reason to fear

11

oppressive laws, or wished to enact some vendetta against powerful people. In any case, the brigands relied for support either on the families that hired them, or the villages from which they came. The desire for survival, which depended on owning a piece of land, at first had drawn many Sicilians toward Garibaldi, who fed the people's hopes and led peasants and many outlaws to coalesce into a guerrilla that fought on his side. But the outcome of Garibaldi's expedition frustrated all hopes and turned those same people against the "Piedmontese" and the very presence of a new State. Brigandage turned into a reactionary force, and a tool in the hands of those who wanted to preserve the status quo. After the 1860s, brigandage matured and set ever deeper roots in those same desperately impoverished lands, now ruled by the new political entity called Italy. After WWI, banditry turned into a cosmopolitan economic and political entity of its own. Its history has intrigued Italian and foreign observers, historians, ethnographers, economists, and sociologists; it has also inspired fictional tales and colorful myths of doubtful accuracy about the outlaws who engaged in it. That mythology then evolved into the unreliable images that today's media propose of a vastly transformed and ruthless universe of organized crime.[3]

*   *

The events of the 1860's are certainly a painful topic for Italians, but they provide a wealth of themes with universal interest to writers: the struggle between idealism and greed, oppression and hunger for liberation, hope for social change and disappointment, political expediency and popular fury. As an Italian of Sicilian extraction, Cutrufelli is very aware of the tormented and rich history of Italy's South, which is the locale of *A Woman Outlaw*[4]. At the same time, she has a worldwide perspective. She weaves the many strands of her experience into the writing of a novel in which "the recreation of historical fact parallels the creation of a female authorial viewpoint that experiences history in both personal and general terms" (Lazzaro-Weis 143).

The originality of the novella lies in the way its main character attempts to fashion her own definition of herself within the context of stories and events greater than herself. All periods of historical rupture allow individuals to go beyond the boundaries of custom that imprison them, and make transgression possible. The protagonist, <u>Margherita</u>, is a young Sicilian woman of the upper class; her personal story begins with a tragic gesture that causes the utter dislocation of her life but also a sort of new birth. In contrast with the other girls of her time and place, she was given an excellent education by her mother, a refined woman from an impoverished aristocratic family who had been raised in a major city. Bound by an arranged marriage to a coarse man who can only imagine a wife to be totally submissive and ignorant, the young woman ends up killing him. Her act challenges a tradition that assigns to men the task of killing, whether to avenge a wrong or obtain freedom. She has placed herself outside the boundary that marks the realm appropriate to her sex and upbringing. After that action, she can only persist in her transgression. She must go into hiding, and she flees to the mountains. Her brother, Cosimo, formerly was a supporter of social change, but now is a member of a band of outlaws that wage a reactionary guerrilla against the forces of the Italian state, after Garibaldi's departure. She finds Cosimo, exchanges her dress for man's clothing, and begins a new life in the woods, at the same time as an observer and a participant in the guerrilla waged by peasant/outlaws. The leader of the band is a former dependent of Cosimo's and Margherita's wealthy landowning family, Carmine Spaziante, a smart and courageous man, who will be defeated by the combination of the superior strength of the regular army and the intricate political alliances of landowners and government.

A vivid narration evokes the daily lives of the men and women brigands, without indulging in myths, sentimentality, or idealization. Margherita experiences hardships and pleasures, fears and desires, gentleness and horror. The figure of the peasant leader, charismatic yet limited and doomed, is drawn in all its forcefulness and contradictions. After several successful actions, the band is decimated and dispersed. Margherita has her life spared but remains confined in a prison from which she will never be freed.

It is difficult to imagine, in our days, the scandal created by a woman's choice to wear masculine clothes, particularly within a closed and traditional society. Lazzaro-Weis and Rossi underline the importance of that transformation in Margherita's appearance by referring to Margherita's "cross-dressing." Whether or not the term is appropriate in this instance, it is clear that the actual moment of Margherita's changing of clothes is a rite of passage akin to other ritual ceremonies that mark a profound change in the wearer's life. Rather than being a mask, as it has been suggested, the new clothes acknowledge the emergence of a part that had remained buried in Margherita's personality. At the end of the novel, when the band is on the run and Margherita is threatened by an armed man, she bares her breasts to reveal the woman under the man's clothing; with that gesture she acknowledges the part of herself that had remained hidden but unmistakeable under her masculine attire.

When she decides to be part of an armed band, Margherita discovers the elation that accompanies the revelation of deeper and complex facets of one's self, but also the ambiguities that go with that complexity. As she participates in the brigand's life, the moments of excitement are followed by horror at the spectacles of ferocity, and dismay at the realization of persisting injustices. Also, the young woman' relations with people outside her own family had until then been ruled by stringent customs. Now she discovers the impact of class boundaries on sexuality as she feels, mixed at first with a sense of surprise and repulsion, the reciprocal attraction between Carmine and herself. She cannot forget the reversal of fortunes that have made him "superior" to her and especially to Cosimo. As for Carmine, he is manly and free in his domain, he is a true leader at the head of a raggedy army, but he remembers with bitterness the barriers that had once kept him in a subservient place. He goes from self-assuredness to clumsiness and from pride to wise reflections, with an ambivalence that is highlighted in the masterful scene of the elegant dinner offered by wealthy landowners to honor the "general" of the brigands ("August 1861").

Gender boundaries are also transgressed when Margherita feels drawn to Antonia, the delicate yet savvy young girl who is Carmine's lover. The ambiguity of Margherita's sensual awakening has as much to do with Antonia's femininity and inclination toward maternal nurturing as it does with Carmine's masculine power. Antonia is Carmine's woman, and Margherita is attracted to both of them because of the couple's obvious reciprocal desire. Margherita is also aware of her own marginal status in the band; she is only accidentally an outlaw. She is unprepared for the brigand's life and unsuited for it because of her upbringing. She is an outsider. The bandits' reasons for fighting are alien to her. Theirs is a class war viscerally lived, which she observes, and participates in, only by choice. She opts for life when faced by certain death because she has realized that the brigands' cause is not her own.

The theme of a woman's construction of her own identity, although never explicitly mentioned, is at the core of Margherita's story and the story of any woman who refuses to stay in the place she has been assigned in the world. It is with admiration that Margherita watches a member of the band, a peasant woman significantly named "Bizzarra" (Strange, and also Untamed One). *La Bizzarra* has fashioned her own destiny to include everything that Margherita admires: fierceness and compassion, healing powers and sensuality, and above all the ability to choose her own definition of herself, not as a brigand's woman but a woman brigand. Maleness and femaleness are shorn in her of their conventional definitions, and it is only logical, in the logic of the story's magic, that she would be the only one to leave the band when it degenerates into an undisciplined horde, and to escape capture. She reappears—invisible under a black veil—perhaps in the flesh, or as a phantom, to lend her strength to Margherita who is brought to the court of justice in chains.

It is significant that Cutrufelli's protagonist, buried in the depths of a prison where she is incarcerated for life, writes her story in the first person. Private writing, from letters to autobiographies and memoirs, has always been the mode available to women for practicing writing and leaving a trace of their own existence and creative imagination in spite of the restrictions imposed on them for centuries. The ambiguous status of certain generic forms is welcome for those who have not been recognized as having a legitimate claim to the construction of traditional forms of history and fiction. Autobiographical writing, whether straightforward or fictional, "is a hybrid and malleable genre that partakes of other genres and becomes a literary space where a woman can experiment with the construction of a female 'I'" (Parati 2). Cutrufelli stated that she chose a well-to-do and educated woman as a protagonist to make it possible for her to speak with a credible voice (Rossi 211-212). Fictional autobiography in fact adds yet another dimension to the complexity of the genre: "The medium of fictional autobiography allows [writers] to exploit fiction to rewrite woman's history from a personal and critical point of view while reaffirming the existence of their own literary tradition" (Lazzaro-Weis *Gendering Italian Fiction* 44). Two voices, therefore, speak in the text, one from a past buried in silence and the other from a present that is interrogating the past and itself.

For it is fiction, ultimately, that comes close to grasping an elusive truth. While the title of the novella underlines the acceptance of a destiny that Margherita transformed into a means for discovering her self and the world around her, the text tells us that her transformation into a conscious human being has taken place only because of her ability to write and her decision to do so in the first person. Born within a prison cell, writing is for Margherita a more profound transgression than murder or brigandage. Indeed, the narrator's and the novelist's simultaneous creation of a written text opens the door to a liberation that is greater than physical freedom. It asserts the presence of self and the preservation of memory. Reflecting on the past truly means living and writing becomes at the same time a means to validate one's own life and to make connection with others. Thus, as we read Margherita's account, we hear not only the voice of an educated woman and the voice of today's writer, but also the echo of those voices that were silenced, of the women who could not leave a record of their own, and yet yearned to survive in someone's memory. Cutrufelli, as the writer she is, asserts through Margherita's voice her trust in the power of writing and in its promise of freedom for those human beings who engage in and with it.

☐

About the Translation

This is the first English translation of Maria Rosa Cutrufelli's *La briganta*. Any translation is an attempt to convey the unique meanings, emotions, sensations, conventions, and mythologies of a culture to which the reader does not have a key. It is the task of the translator to make that unfamiliar culture accessible through a new medium that is faithful to its own music and traditions.

Cutrufelli proposes an additional difficulty: she writes in the first person a fictional memoir penned by a nineteenth-century, well-educated woman of the Sicilian upper class. The medium she elaborates is a flawlessly clear twentieth-century Italian with a well calibrated touch of nineteenth-century flavor, appropriate to the personal writing of a woman of that time and place. The translator has attempted to imitate her technique by keeping in mind the examples of fiction written by nineteenth-century American women.

1 Martin Clark's concise history of *Risorgimento* is a valuable introduction to the topic, although one must disregard its patronizing subtext; see Chapter 8, "The Unification of Italy" (75-100). Denis Mack Smith translated and edited a useful collection of primary sources in *The Making of Italy* (see especially pages 307-352); see also pages 1-26 and 58-83 of his *Modern Italy*. Villari's *Il Sud nella storia d'Italia* is an essential anthology of primary sources; and Renda's "La rivoluzione del 1860" and "La restaurazione liberal-moderata" (145-212) in his *Storia di Sicilia* are the best sources for this topic. See also Romeo's moderate and optimistic interpretation of the same events in "L'unificazione" (346-382) in his *Il Risorgimento in Sicilia*.

2 The most illustrious items of evidence are the *canzone* "*All'Italia*" by Francesco Petrarca, echoed five centuries later by a young Giacomo Leopardi's own *canzone*; and Niccolò Machiavelli's passionate call for a prince to bring about Italy's deliverance (*The Prince* XXVI).

3 All histories of the *Risorgimento* in Southern Italy devote considerable space to this phenomenon. In recent years this topic is usually, and improperly, addressed under the heading "mafia," for which there are over five hundred entries in the catalogue of the Library of Congress for just the last tirty years or so.

4 For this novel, see Monica Rossi's article that includes an interview with the author.

The more life is filled with privation, hardship, and sorrow, the more we cling to it.

I am entombed alive. Twenty years have I already spent here! And twenty years of a life sentence are more eternal than death. And death only will put an end to this eternal vigil. Yet, every day I strive to live on, quelling all emotion and desire incompatible with the condition of the living dead. And within the emptiness of my mind, within my body that is dulled to feeling and seems almost to have thickened, I search incessantly for something: the glimmer of a memory, the eye of another woman prisoner that suddenly comes alive, something that might reawaken me. Each one of us, inside these walls, labors to recapture a sense of herself in the ceaseless wasting of Time, be it through an illness, or pain, or violence. Anything is an occasion to recover one emotion, one emotion at least, to make one's heart beat faster once again.

My opportunity has come. I, who during the trial uttered not a word, now wish to be heard. I want my voice to go forth from the cell that imprisons my body. Today I am allowed this escape: I have paper, ink, a pen, and a story to tell, a past to resurrect from the depths of my own oblivion. One day, perhaps, someone will understand how this may be more intoxicating than an actual escape, what enormous freedom it is to speak, at last. And then, it may be that silence will again bury me and engulf my mind; and thoughts and words will become the scattered and useless fragments of a broken plaything.

Until yesterday, I lived a prisoner of the present. My memories inhabited my dreams and nightmares, and opening my heart to the future was a crime. Now, unexpectedly, Time has opened up again before me; I am free to speak in my own voice to other human beings, and to engage in intercourse with equals. Those who will read me, indeed, will be moved by a desire to know and to know me, not to judge and punish, and in such wish for knowledge we will be equals.

We live in a century thirsting for progress and science, and it is to men of science I owe this redemption that lay beyond hope. At times, during these many years, their behavior appeared to me cruel and incomprehensible. In the infirmary and in their laboratories, they measured innumerable times the circumference of my head, with a meticulous curiosity. They made complicated calculations on my person: they measured the length of my arms, my eyesight, my reflexes, my hearing, my touch, and my sensitivity to pain... All the while they complained because in the Kingdom of Italy—so they said—it is forbidden to study properly delinquent people and to carry through exams and laboratory experiments. Ah, if science could only have the freedom it enjoys in Russia and other civilized nations! The goal of those men was not, as I knew immediately, to understand illness and heal the flesh. As they told me nothing, I was terrified at first; my imagination ran wild and I, paralyzed by horror, was incapable of responding in the manner of a human being. I was a dumb creature frightened to death. As time went on, I understood. Those men were intent on finding in the body the traces of emotions, as if they were a snail's dribble. They truly believed that the secret of human ferocity and malice could be found hidden in the measurements of my poor cranium.

Much later—I do not know how much later, years, centuries— I had a different visitor. The man who came to my cell cultivates not only science, but pity also. He is a historian, who is more interested in my words than in the obstinately mute wretchedness of my body, which is now only a shadow of what it once was, anyhow. Our philosophers have often decried History as untrustworthy and useless, it being knowledge of what was done once and not of what must be done. Dispenser of ancient prejudices and teacher of errors and crimes, that is the manner they defined it, forgetting that History is also the record of a passionate search for the paths of justice, a search concretely abiding in the experiences of human beings.

The events of my life, it is true, are unwonted and not edifying. The record regarding my trial was in fact what moved that scholarly man. My silence surprised him more than my wrongdoings. He learned that I was still living, buried in this penitentiary, and wished to become acquainted with me.

20

I received him wrapped in a suspicious and hostile diffidence. He returned again, many times, without forcing me to speak, explaining with a quiet eloquence what he expected from me; the gentleness of his obstinacy at last moved me and won me over. I was beginning to be tempted by the endeavor. I told him my story in brief, and I believed that his participation was sincere, although I could see that in truth what moved him was more the emotion of the man than the interest of the scholar. For the man of science I was but an anomaly to note, a queerness of History. To this day, I do not know how far he may have believed in the usefulness of my testimony. He has taken a lot of trouble to obtain for me the permission to write my memoirs, but it is uncertain how much he was spurred by pity, and how much by the conviction that I may have something to tell to everyone and for everyone.

I know that many others who are now like me buried alive and once were outlaws like me, in those remote years, have written or—since most all of them are illiterate—have dictated their memoirs, and he has gathered them in order that those confessions may serve the cause of History. But can a woman move and interest an audience of men, for such I fancy to be the readership of these pages? I realize the folly of this project, and some people will find in it further proof and confirmation that folly inspired my entire life. For a woman, to write her memoirs is a bold act, perhaps even bolder that roaming the mountains as an outlaw. Do not assume, seeing as I prepare to speak about myself, that I am proud of my past, of the choices I made, and my actions; far from it. God is my witness. And yet...If I were granted today an improbable grace, would I quit this prison corrected and reformed? I wish to be sincere: I do not know. Resignation causes me to say that I sinned and must expiate. But what about repentance?

Surely, this last folly, writing my story, is a sin of pride; and the power of this sin sets afire my soul and my face. This acknowledgement will please the scientist armed with measuring tools, and the ethnologists of crime who studied me so painstakingly. It confirms a theory of theirs, which I heard them utter so many times, that women may commit fewer crimes, but when they do so they are more cruel and obstinate, and less given to repentance, than the most ferocious and hardened of men.

Thinking back over the events of my life I acknowledge that I acted, and even now I am acting, under the impulse of strong feelings, which defeated the resistance of my body and that of my spirit. I forgot, as I gave in on those impulses, that I am a woman.

*   *

Every memoir begins with a name. Mine is Margherita. And my readers must be content with my own name, my first name. I have already involved the name of my family excessively, and with too much sorrow, in scandals and shame. Besides, of what help is the name, in this circumstance, but to allow an identification as useless as it is malevolent?

You must know, however, that my mother belonged to a family of aristocratic descent, though wealthier in daughters than in riches. She was the sixth child; the seventh was a male, who inherited whatever there was to be inherited. Though lacking a dowry, my mother was a good match for any gentleman in the provinces, and she was married to my father, who was not noble but was a wealthy owner of cultivated land and woods, farms and country dwellings.

A strange destiny is what brought me, born rich and of a noble family on my mother's side, to share the fate of so many children of the wretched poor! But I am not seeking pity for the path I chose; I seek compassion for a courage I used unwisely. The question is whether a different use of it was possible. Courage is a superfluous virtue in a woman, a virtue that we steal from man and becomes, perhaps inevitably, vice and despair.

My hometown, where I lived peacefully until the age of twenty two, is small, hidden in the pool of shade formed by a circle of mountains, and surrounded by the silence of scarcely farmed fields. Such were many towns in the former Kingdom of the Two Sicilies. Ignorant of hates and injustices, I used to spend my time with serenity, raised with certain pretentions — or, to speak more forthrightly, with a certain conceitedness — by a mother who had been born and educated in the faraway capital of the Kingdom. She was a woman

22

who had been admired and courted for her mind and culture, as well as for her beauty which was perfectly in keeping with her spirit: she was blond, fragile, and with eyes so clear that they made her glance elusive. She held a salon, when she was young, which was frequented by poets and brilliant officers, philosophers and famous lawyers, politicians and economists. Those were years she could not forget. How could one forget the company of men of intellect and experience, men who had seen the republican revolution of 1799, and still discussed the tragedy of the Neapolitan Republic? A painter had made pastel portraits of those famous guests who were most assiduous frequenters of her salon — he was one of them — and she had kept the portraits in an album, which she often leafed through with me, as she recounted their stories.

My father was very dissimilar from her. To him, only the aristocratic lineage of the woman he had married mattered, and for that he tolerated even her extravagances. First among them was having given me some education; a truly unwonted thing in our parts, where girls are usually not even taught to write out of fear that they might correspond with lovers. And the few who can read are allowed only prayer-books and the lives of saints. Mine, on the contrary, was a true education, although my mother chose for my instruction an old teacher from town, because she did not want to send me to boarding school far away. When the teacher had taught me all she could teach, my mother took my education into her own hands. She would read me memoirs and the histories of remote men and countries, or she recited from memory short and long poems, in the stifling afternoons when the sun lingered forever high in the sky, and we dreamed of the coolness of evening while our hands were busy with needlework. The shutters, half-closed, filtered the violent light, which fell only on the looms and on the soft silk embroidery, the red, blue, and bright silver of the threads. I was proud of my mother and, because of her, I was proud of myself. I held myself fortunate, and I do so to this day, in spite of all that has happened. And yet, my fate should convince me of the opposite. My fate supports my husband's pronouncements; he affirmed with greater heat than necessary that women's hearts and brains are ruined by the alphabet, literature promotes doubts that our mediocrity is not up to solving, and the shoemaker must be content with his awl as woman must be with her loom.

My mother's death caught me unawares, leaving me bewildered, with a sense of emptiness and solitude that only my brother Cosimo could have filled. But Cosimo was studying in the capital, and he returned home rarely, only for an occasional short visit. He liked life in the city, though in recent years the inconveniences and the dishonesty of the Borbonic police had become more pronounced. All the students were expected to have a residency document that the police could renew or deny every month; they had to attend mass, listen to sermons, sing at the services, and go to confession. The religious congregation of which all the students had to be members issued a certificate of attendance, without which one could not take exams. All that notwithstanding, Cosimo loved the city and his student life.

Therefore, I lived practically alone with my father, who seemed vexed, and impatient of my presence. He would linger for ever longer periods of time in the country, in some remote farm, with his peasant lovers. He did not act thus because of lack of affection. The fact was that he had assigned a precise position to me and to my brother in the pattern of his existence. He had chosen that position as one decides on the placing of furnishings. He had arranged us in the appropriate corner, and he had left us there with entire tranquillity of mind. I did not suffer because of such estrangement; things had always been thus. And yet that was a period of painful melancholy for me. I had lost all my assurance, I felt empty and devoid of emotions, and deprived of any support. My father's impatience humiliated me profoundly. I agreed to his giving me in marriage. One day someone knocked at the main door. A smiling maid of mature age brought a gift of sweets on a monumental tray. It was the opening of the marriage negotiations, in accordance with our customs.

I knew nothing of reality and life; my mother had taught me to read and daydream, but not to defend myself. I lacked all experience of the world, of men, and of men's dealings. My father, when it came to the clauses of the marriage contract, was concerned about the patrimony, but "patrimony" was a word devoid of interest, and even of meaning, for me.

24

My husband began to undo what my mother had built.

After my wedding, I had transferred to my new residence our rich family library. It contained rare books, which hardly circulated in the provinces, and had for the greater part been ordered or personally purchased by my mother. There might be leaflets that had escaped the Jesuits' censorship, or foreign books imported illegally from Naples and Palermo, when that particular contraband was a dangerous and difficult activity but also very profitable. There were newspapers printed by the opposition, which had appeared all of a sudden the day Ferdinand II had sworn allegiance to the Constitution and had granted freedom of the press. Seeing those papers, my husband trembled. It was April 1860, and the future of the Kingdom, the future of Italy, was still very uncertain. My husband had liberal inclinations, but was cautious in his acts. The dangerous papers disappeared. There still remained to me my best loved books, of poetry and literature. During the patron saint's festivities, my husband gave them also away, to be used for the fireworks. I said nothing, perhaps I even agreed, as I had agreed to my marriage. Two young boys came to take the books away, and left all bent under sacks made of rough cloth. I escorted them back to the front door. The bouquets that opened up brightly in the sky a few nights later fell back all rotted in my heart.

Neither books nor music had a part any more in my new married life. No space was found for the player piano that my mother also had loved so much; it remained abandoned in a corner of the entrance hall.

* *

But what am I bringing back to memory? I am not writing to accuse anyone, or to seek vengeance for the wrongs done to me, whether they are imagined or real. Why am I writing, then? One only is my intention, one only my goal: to feel alive once again, perhaps for the last time, to feel alive in the mere resurfacing of memories, but also in the attempt to reflect and know myself in memory's mirror.

Where must I start from? I have reflected at length on this matter. And I think and hope that a woman buried alive may be allowed a sincerity of expression that would otherwise be unbecoming and even unnatural. The temptation and the pleasure to express oneself freely are powerful when one cannot act in freedom any more; but freedom of expression is not easy. I am reminded again, in this instance, of the words said by the measuring-prone scientists. Stealing and deceiving—they used to say—are not in themselves an indication of great perversity in a woman. Respect for property rights is not among woman's strongest feelings, therefore no great degeneracy is needed to lose it. But modesty, ah! modesty, after the maternal instinct, is the most powerful feeling in woman; the entire psychic evolution of woman has been working for centuries with utter energy to create and strengthen that feeling.

Indeed, that is true. How difficult it is to break down, and more so with words, those barriers that for centuries have made our own hearts mysterious to us. Modesty, reserve—what scissors will cut the bars of such cages, and show us such as we are, human beings before other human beings. As for me, I feel that a most fierce blade has operated on me with its sturdy and malefic metal. In any event, men's final judgement has placed my person beyond all anxiety or earthly caution, and in fear only of God's judgement. Modesty also, which is necessary only to those who live in human society, has died in me. And reticence is a luxury I do not want, nor can allow myself; what I will not say now will be said never more.

I will begin with the day that stamped my life for ever with its mark of blood.

I felt calm, and mistress of my emotions. My hands only, which had been, just a short time earlier, so steady and assured, trembled so hard that I was not able to control them. I ceased to attempt dressing, and I sat again on the bed turning my back to the body of my husband. The silence in the room, which was not broken but by my breathing, spread a fog on my mind. That stillness, it was that stillness that made his body heavier with every passing moment, and though I had my face turned to the wall I could see it and perceive its malignant power that paralyzed me.

The brick that Filomena had placed at the foot of the bed to warm the bed linens, since it was still cold in the evenings, had slipped to the floor. I noticed then that it was scored by deep and intricate crevices the same pattern and color of my old servant's face.

"I always hated this room, it is gloomy"—I said aloud, shaken by a senseless rage, and I pushed into a corner, with my foot, the brick that was by now cold.—"I must move. I must leave," I murmured afterwards, in an effort to urge myself on. It was tempting to lie down and let myself be slowly stifled by that heavy and still body that turned to stone everything about it, even the very air. And yet, I recoiled from the vision of being found thus, almost stupefied, and without strength or purpose. I recoiled above all from the idea of having before me familiar, domestic faces, and being searched by their incredulous and questioning eyes. Spikes of red hot iron, they were ready to probe my breast. And I should speak, explain... No, not that, they cannot force me, I thought.

Suddenly, a cold breath brushed my neck. I jumped up terrified. The room, in its darkness barely dispelled by the votive lamp on the chest of drawers, was immobile in its accustomed order. And his body, laid on its back, took up, as it was accustomed, the entire right hand of the bed, with arms open and abandoned in a deathly inertia. I turned my face away quickly, yet the glimmering of the silver hatpin in his bare throat burned my eyes. It is a done deed— I thought—it is done. And now? Apathy again enveloped me. I felt empty and tired as for an excessive fatigue. I felt like fleeing, or at least quitting that room, but my legs were torpid and weak so that I feared they might not support me.

A faraway noise roused me; it came perhaps from the end of the alley, and I was not able to identify it. I did not know if it bode ill or well. Filomena would have known, she would have understood at once which way fate was leading. I resolved to go, and in order to stifle the trembling that still shook me I wrapped myself tightly in the woolen cape I had carelessly abandoned on the wood chest. It covered me from head to foot. The Virgin of the Seven Sorrows was smiling melancholically from the top of the chest of drawers. I approached it, dipped the tip of my fingers in the lamp's oil, and— remembering an old superstition—I passed my fingers over my forehead. The oil's persistent warmth gave me a strange sense of comfort.

The hall turned out to seem very long, gelid and alien like the first time I had entered that house. Exactly one year had gone by since that day. The room of my mother-in-law was at the end of the corridor, somewhat out of the way, but the uneven, laboured sound of her old woman's snoring filled it. Her door was ajar and I slowed down as I passed it. She would probably be the first to find him. At a certain hour she would enter our bedroom perplexed and worried. Yes, I would have wished to see it, that old face of hers, hard and thin as a blade, from which Time with its claws had erased all trace of benevolence, however minute. Hateful thoughts assailed me and lashed my blood, making it run in my veins with the same force that had guided my hand a short time earlier. In the atrium, near the main door that opened onto the street, sat my old player piano; I had never opened it in that house. I felt the sting of nostalgia pierce me. Never again will I open it up—I thought. The main door was barred, and I knew that I would not be able to open it without noise. I ran back, climbed on tiptoes the stairs that led to the kitchen, and from there I descended the external steps that went into the garden. When I closed the door, I felt I had locked inside the humid and cold breath that ran on my traces from one side to the other of the house. The night darkness was comforting, and I immersed myself in it as if in a warm and calm water. The house, behind me, was a receding nightmare.

The road led away from the populated area toward a countryside that was deserted at that hour of the night. It was a fortunate happenstance that I did not have to cross the entire town; my husband's mansion rose almost at its entrance, leaning onto an ancient city wall. I did not use caution to hide, for the night extended me its protection. Right outside the town a path crossed the road and led to the public wash-house, grey-stoned and covered by a hanging roof. By now, the houses were not visible any more. A ravine opened by the side of the road, and the river bed ran white at the bottom. In the distance, there was the massive darkness of the mountains, and the silhouette of the wash-house rose as imposing as a monument of bizarre construction, a dwelling of malignant spirits who liked to stir the dormant waters of the tubs. I moved with uneasy and suspicious steps followed by the fantastic remembrance of old time legends. No concrete fear, no emotion stirred me at that moment, but ghostly breaths. I touched my forehead still damp with the oil, and quickened my pace. At the crossroad, I turned decisively toward the mountains.

* *

At this point, my remembrance becomes confused. When the trees became thicker and the woods began, the sudden sensation of danger made me pause for an instant. Darkness was becoming more dense and heavier before me. At each of my movements I had the impression that a black abyss rent the earth under my feet. I was terrified, but an anguished frenzy impelled me to go forward, it did not matter where. Whether it was day or night was indifferent to me because I had the impression that I had gone blind and deaf. Life had stopped in the woods, and I felt only the aching of my blood pulsing in the veins of my temples and wrists, as in a fever attack.

The sun awoke me, and I kept my eyes closed for a long time savoring its reassuring caress. My head was unencumbered and free at last. The scent of trees and earth penetrated through the linen of my long shirt and the wool of my cape. I remember vividly the strangeness of that awakening that filled entirely my body and my mind, and the morning light that shone directly in my eyes but without violence. Violence was in the remembrance of the closed, stagnating air of the bedroom. Every morning in that long, long year, waking up had been agony. I could not become accustomed to that body stretched by mine, a body that slowly consumed all the air of the room at night, depriving me even of a space for dreaming. Indeed, I did not dream any more.

I was always the first to rise, and I went up to the big kitchen, dark even in the summer. The smell of milk boiling slowly, the dry throat cough of Filomena, the old servant I had brought from my father's house, marked a pause that lasted little, but made me feel again like myself. I thought: today there will be no smell of milk, the fireplace will not be lit, and the main door will remain barred. Mourning will inhabit that house in perpetuity. And fragments of other memories began mingling with the remembrance of those morning awakenings, which I pushed at once back to the depths of my mind. Not yet—I would tell myself—not yet. I did not feel strong enough to face reality, the weight of that final, irreparable gesture. The trees surrounded me and impeded the view of the horizon; in the distance you could hear the dripping from wet leaves. It had perhaps rained somewhere.

I stood up, impelled by the unaccustomed restlessness that mechanically moved my feet. At first I followed the path. My steps echoed with a dull, obsessive sound on the beaten track, so I started to walk in the thickness of the woods. The shrubs clinged to my cape and scratched my hands; the path became ever more impervious; I sank in the dead leaves and thick underbrush. But the harder became the resistance I had to overcome, the greater was the relief I felt. The light rained from up high like a miracle, shining suddenly on leaves that the rain or the dew had drenched. I felt that I was mistress of my time. I was inebriated, I walked with steps that suddenly were light, carried forth by my own lightness. I was neither hungry nor thirsty; I was too taken with living through a time that was not measured any more by every day habits and gestures. The daily rhythm of life had broken down forever.

When I looked around, I had the impression that I was lost, but that did not worry me. It was the first time I was in the heart of the mountains alone, and yet I felt no fear. I moved with assurance remembering my brother's words and advice. Cosimo had often taken me along in his protracted, solitary hikes. We spoke but little. He broke the silence now and then to tell me the names of the places, to point out a tree, or a leaf, or the tracks of an animal. After that, he had gone to the city to study, and I...I had married.

The mountain stream already swollen by the spring floods blocked my path. It ran deep and swift between narrow rock ledges, but further down it widened spreading on a dazzling shingle, an oasis of light. I recognized the place. Without being conscious of it, I had retraced the very paths I had so often travelled with Cosimo, I had walked along mule-tracks, and climbed shortcuts we had so often taken together. And I had been unconscious of it until that moment. I stopped as if struck by lightning: I was certain now, I had been looking for my brother. It was on his traces that I had started. Ad yet, I did not know where to look for him. I knew only that the woods were also his shelter, since he was a fugitive, not a student any more but a soldier of King Francesco, as they used to say then. Or, an outlaw, as they said later.

*　*

Everything had begun little more than a year earlier, at the time of the Red Shirts' May expedition, and the insurrection. The news of the landing of a small band of men, Garibaldi's "One Thousand," had not spread yet, and already a kingdom was collapsing with the slow, dull crash of a landslide down a mountainside.

All of Italy had long been seething. In the North, a new state was in the process of forming around Piedmont and the "Honest King." In the South, a thousand dark intrigues and a thousand different interests were weaving a web together to bring about the collapse of the Bourbons. In my town also, far in the midst of the mountains, there were conspiracies. At the apothecary, in the evenings, people did not play cards any more, and instead of exchanging gossip, as they used to, all the good and honorable men had suddenly become politicians.

And then, all of a sudden, Garibaldi, the Dictator, was on the continent. He advanced rapidly and the liberals opened up the way for him while the populace was seduced with the most improbable promises: no more conscription, no more taxes. Those were the benefits touted by the new Italian government. And the mirage of owning one's own land.

When the mirage dissolved, blood began to flow. As Francesco II abandoned Naples to take refuge in the Gaeta fortress in a vain attempt at resistance, the peasants, the *cafoni,* were burning on the squares the effigy of Garibaldi, the traitor. When the cold weather arrived, the news of the plebiscite was heard. The people were to vote with universal suffrage (universal for the males, the women not being included) in favor of an "Italy one and indivisible, with Victor Emmanuel II and his descendants as its constitutional kings." The vote was open because there were two ballot boxes, one for the yes votes and one for the no votes, but the voting halls controlled by armed men, and the guns in the hands of the poll watchers certainly did little to serve the people's rights and freedom of conscience.

That was the manner in which Italy was united. We forgot about it for some time, once the snows separated us from the rest of the world.

It was at the beginning of that melancholic and ominous winter that Cosimo returned home. He had left many months before with some other students to join the insurrection and to enlist in Garibaldi's army as a volunteer. It was a natural and inevitable choice. Ever since he had been a student in the city, my brother had been attracted by subversive ideas. During his brief visits he spoke of nothing but the peoples' awakening, the collapse of the thrones, and the clamor of barricades. Hearing those words, which were in such contrast with the deathly silence enveloping my new life, gave me a satisfaction, a strange gladness that entranced me.

Cosimo returned a November afternoon. And he informed me that the Southern contingent of Garibaldi's volunteers had beeen disbanded, and that many of his friends were in despair and at a loss, without bread or money in their pockets, and without any future. They had applied to enter the regular army, but their applications were almost invariably rejected. He told me about the fear that troubled their consciences, and about the bitterness that poisoned their thoughts and clouded even the most lucid minds. He also had been discharged.

32

He said no more that day. And yet I was not surprised when I learned that, having met the band led by Carmine Spaziante, who had once been farm overseer for our father, he had joined it. From Garibaldi volunteer he had become Francesco's soldier, from a Republican to a defender of legitimism. My father, when that news reached him, went straight to the gun rack, took down a gun, charged it, and with a cold rage climbed on his horse. "I will drive out that snake"—he screamed at the terrified stable hand—"I will find him, and I will drain him of all his poison." They restrained him by force.

Ice gripped the days between 1860 and 1861 as in a vise. It was a particularly long and cold winter, and the roofs of several houses in the farmhands' quarter fell under the weight of the snow. I was thinking of all those who had gone into hiding, of Cosimo, and the white, still silence of the woods made me insane with anguish. Then the slow dripping of water from the gutters announced the spring thaw.

*　　*

I remained without stirring during I do not know how long a time, looking at the stream that foamed spreading among the stones. Then, all of a sudden, the echo of excited and almost breathless voices reached my ears. I plunged again into the woods. Until night fell again, slowly, imperceptibly. And I had again my dreams, as intense and vivid as hallucinations. When I awoke, my first thought went again to Filomena. She was the confidant of all my girlish dreams, and in the winter evenings, with our feet close to the brazier, she would repeat them to me, explaining them, interpreting them, and weaving again the story of my life with new threads, those of predictions and visions.

I sat up. The earth was damp at the touch, and my hair, all undone, fell in an untidy mass on my face. I raised my arm to pin it back, and was struck by a flash of remembrance: the hairpin that had fallen from my hair on the pillow, and the resolution that had burst inside me with the overpowering violence of a scream; the initial resistance of the flesh quickly overcome; his breath, heavy with sleep, that became a raucous gurgling, a jerking motion, and the uncontrolled trembling of the body. I looked in disbelief at my hands, my thin wrists, and felt again a retching in my throat. I wished

33

at that moment for Filomena's dry, resentful cough, the warm water in the enameled basin, and my slow lingering before the mirror.

And yet, not being able to go back, that reassured me. No remorse, no weakness could ever give me back my previous life, and my act itself, in its madness, belonged to another time, another world. Or, perhaps, it was the beginning of something new. But what new time, what new world could I enter now? A weariness that was not caused by my exertions and fasting but came from further back, a very long way back, arose within me and grew rapidly. It was a wave that moved in from the horizon and ran toward me growing ever higher, ever more swollen. And at last it overcame me.

I felt that I was not going to rise ever again, and with a sigh of relief I let myself fall back. In that instant, appearing out of nowhere, I saw Cosimo coming toward me. Tall, dressed in black cloth in the peasant fashion, he wore the Bourbons' lily embroidered on his cap.

* *

I regained my senses in a small windowless room that was lit by the smoky flame of an oil lamp. There were packing cases along the wall, a pile of wood, and a strong musty odor of cheese and herbs. The bed was large and comfortable. The pleasure of sinking my head in a pillow and stretching my legs under the blanket was intense, but it did not prevent me from noticing the incongruity of that comfortable bed in a room that was without any doubt used for the storage of goods. I remembered little or nothing of the road we had taken to get to the farm, but Cosimo's arms around me.

Cosimo was seated nearby with his eyes lost far away. His face looked tired. The flickering light accentuated the shadows around his eyes, and drew more markedly the lines on both sides of his mouth, instead of erasing them. He was young, my brother, hardly a year older than I was. And yet, in the anguish of that night watch, his youthfulness was a thin mask that let through, as if in transparency, the heavy marks of old age. It was a face of his that I did not know and turned him into a stranger for me.

There had always been much closeness between me and Cosimo, a greater intimacy than is customary between brother and sister in our land, where rapports between people are rigid and formal. Even as adults, we had continued to address each other infor-

34

mally, and our father was irritated by it, judging that behavior a personal affront, as if we wanted to remind him, with such unseemly habit, of the lusterless origins of his own family.

Cosimo and I had been bound by a reassuring and spontaneous trust; and now I did not dare any more to call to my brother, I did not dare to break a silence that felt alien, if not hostile. I wanted to speak to him, and yet I still hesitated, with my arms weakly abandoned on the covers. Then our eyes met and his face was once again the face of the handsome young man I loved.

He only asked: "Are you thirsty?" I drank anxiously and greedily. My lips were dry and cracked, and they burned. I drank without catching my breath, leaning on him. The coolness of the water and the closeness of his body made me shiver and reacquire a sense of reality. I did not need to speak, because Cosimo said: "You have had a fever for two days. You were delirious, but now...."

He pronounced each word with care, almost fearing that I might not be able to understand them yet. In truth, my weakness made me dizzy. I kept leaning on him, a hand on his arm, subjugated by the strength I could sense under those rough clothes that I was not accustomed to seeing him wear. A vague and remote unease was mixed with the sense of relief that his presence inspired in me. I wished I could abandon myself in his comforting embrace as I had abandoned myself to the fever, a few moments before. But I understood that it was not possible to do so anymore, and that he expected...what did he expect? Panic made me tongue-tied and drained my mind. I could find no words and no thoughts. It was Cosimo who again broke our silence, and a vague fright quivered in his voice: "It was not easy to find you."

The room had a tile floor. Near the bed there was a crucifix made of wood, and on the same nail hanged palm leaves worked into a chalice and a dried, dusty olive branch. In spite of the drink of water, my throat was still dry and my tongue was swollen. I felt as if my eyes were bleeding, they were burning so as I looked ardently into my brother's face. He did not dare to move away, and did not dare to touch me, perplexed and intimidated by the intensity of my look. "I will not abandon you,"—he told me—"you can be sure of it."

35

I realized then that he was afraid. But of what was he afraid? What made his eyes avoid me, and his hands hesitant? He was looking at me as if he had difficulty recognizing me, and still he attempted to reassure me.

"Do not fear"—and his voice was quick, slightly agitated.—"I will take you away immediately. To the monastery of Longapietra, you know it...The Mother Superior is a woman of great intelligence and compassion. We will decide with her what to do, and until we have decided you will be safe inside the monastery."

I could not say what I had expected, nor what I wanted from him, but I did not expect those words, surely not those words. What told me as much was the bitter astonishment that rose in my throat like bile, and my body that turned to ice. His words had been a violent blow. I did understand instantly that his proposal was wise. Why then did a wave of suppressed weeping weigh on my breast? I could count on Cosimo, on Cosimo and on his help. Was it not because of it that I had looked for him, albeit unawares, moving like an automaton in a nightmare? Cosimo was defending me without asking for anything, without asking me even a question. He stood between me and the world, taking my destiny in his hands as if I were a little girl crushed by a tragic fatality. That is how he wanted to see me. And what troubled him was his very condition of fugitive, of outlaw, which prevented him from protecting me entirely and becoming a shield between me and reality. Pity, worry, and his desire to reassure me altered his features. I should have been grateful to him for his being on my side in such a total, unconditional way. But the tears that veiled my eyes were tears of impotence. Everything had been in vain, then: such was the unexpected reflection that went through my mind.

Someone had spread over the covers my grey cape, which was torn in several points. I was looking at those tears and could feel the thorns of the bushes stabbing my flesh and tearing my skin. I felt in my very body the night's wounds. Cosimo's urge to protect me took my responsibilities away from me, carried me back, and made me an impotent, passive spectator of my own life. That was precisely what I did not wish. The comforting and compassionate grip of his hands felt like a vise from which I freed myself with an involuntary wrench.

He fixed his eyes on me, amazed and alarmed. And at that moment I made my decision, at last free to make a choice. Now, for the first time in my life, it was imperative that I be free to make a choice, or all the suffering endured would have been in vain.

My voice was still weak but clear. Cosimo, however, did not grasp the meaning of my words at first, and I had to repeat slowly: "I am staying, I am staying here with you."

The surprise made him dizzy. He still had his hand on my shoulder, and he pulled it back with a brusk movement as if he had been scalded. Then I read in his eyes a new feeling, an understanding that was dawning with difficulty. It was not pleasant. He was truly looking at me for the first time since he had rescued me in the woods. I felt him distant physically, though his hand was once again resting on my shoulder, procuring me pain but also relief. And under that sense of relief a flame of rancor rose within me, still hidden but spreading like fire that snakes through the grass. Rancor for what, and against whom, I would be unable to say.

* *

The door opened right at that moment. My immediate reaction was one of dismay, and I retreated in fright toward the bed. From far in the distance, men's voices reached my ear, and then a brief call rang cheerfully from the next room. A woman came in carrying a steaming bowl.

As long as I live I shall remember that first encounter with Antonia. Antonia D'Acquisto, that was the name of Carmine Spaziante's lover; he was the band's leader. But I didn't know those things then.

The smoky glow of the oil lamp and the feeble daylight that came through the door that was wide open barely allowed me to make out the young woman, who was standing hesitating at the threshold. What struck me above all was her blond hair and the dazzling smile playing on her lips. At first glance, I had the impression that she could not be more than thirteen or fourteen, a little girl who was making a votive offering through the

37

fragrant smoke of the oil lamp. "Ah, Filomena—I thought—this is indeed a good omen."

"Carmine sends his greetings, donna Margherita. Would you like a little broth? You must be hungry." A gentle, naive face bent toward me. Nothing could trouble or contradict the trusting openness of that smile. I was astonished. For certain, I did not expect to meet a woman in that place and at that moment. As I looked upon that young and serene face, I felt all tension release and my tiredness return. But now I could abandon myself; her small hands lifted me with more experience and sureness than Cosimo's strong hands. Yes, I was hungry. No sooner had I taken the first gulp than I felt a stabbing pain in my stomach, and sweat poured down my back. Patiently, the girl put the bowl down on the floor, wiped my face with a white cloth that she pulled out of her bodice, and then raised again the bowl to my lips. Overcoming my trembling, I started to drink slowly.

I drank the broth in small sips from the cup she held with one hand while with her other hand she kept holding me up, and I felt the warmth of her breast on my cheek. I was again littlle and trusting, and I was drinking life from her. With cautious but avid and determined gulps I was drinking my fate. I raised my eyes only when I had finished every drop. And I realized then that Cosimo had left the room.

*   *

It was in that manner that I chose the reactionary forces, I who had been stirred by patriotic readings and the noble ideals of the country's resurrection and unity. By choosing the mountains, I had unwittingly chosen reaction. Events are opaque while we live them, and they do not allow us to be fully aware of our actions. One gesture, one gesture only, and we are unable to stop the thousand rivulets that draw their origin from that first source. Never would I have believed that I would have been drawn to make such a choice. I had dreamed of Italy, the Constitution, and the end of absolute monarchy and tyranny. But when the dream had turned into reality, I had joined the forces of reaction. Such was the name given to legitimism, and at the same time to the peasants' uprisings, which the Bourbons, in those years, tried to bring under their white flag. Those were lost years, the years of my youth, so bitterly lost.

With the coming of spring, the bands thinned out by winter used to swell up again, like the rivers. The same happened with Carmine Spaziante's band, a small army of about three hundred people, which was augmented every day by new faces and unfamiliar voices. The major part were peasants, daily laborers who despaired of ever finding work, or young men who had fled the draft. At times they would arrive barefoot and unarmed, as if the band's quarters were a magnet, an irresistible, fated attraction. But there were also soldiers from the Bourbons' army, most miserable and desperate of all, because they possesssed but their old uniforms and their unbending concept of obedience and iron discipline. Some of them came from Gaeta; they had escaped before the city's surrender in order to avoid imprisonment and to continue fighting in the mountains. They exhibited with pride a medal-souvenir they had been given, and recounted the glorious and terrible siege, stories of privations, suffering, and deadly fevers. But the king and the queeen—the queen especially, beautiful and courageous—had never failed to be among them. No one had been able to sleep during the entire time of the siege, so bright was the night under the continuous fire of rifled cannons, a new and deadly weapon that the godless Piedmontese army had first tried out against the Gaeta fortress. The projectiles had such power of penetration that they could go through a mountain from side to side. Vainly did the black flags fly over hospitals and temporary shelters for the wounded and the sick; the rain of fire forgave nothing and no one.

The other men, the peasants, the new soldiers of King Francesco who were wearing shepherds' sandals called *cioce* and brigands' hats, just listened. They disbelieved only one thing, that the tales of sufferings they were hearing could have surpassed those they themselves had withstood. Many among them had spent the winter in the mountains, alone or in small bands, keeping as close as possible to their home villages to be able to replenish their victuals and armaments through family and friends, according to the ancient tradition of brigandage. But the men in hiding were many that year, more numerous and famished than the wolves. Their providers were poor peasants and destitute shepherds, as they were, and had to ration bread to their own children.

The country estate around which the band had gathered belonged to a rich man who had acquired little by little, field after field, house after house, all the possessions of the prince who, not much earlier, had been the sole owner of all the land around. Carmine Spaziante would laugh inside his thick curly beard: "What a hand he has! What he sees he gets. He is like Judas. He flirts with the liberals in the city, but look what a good host he is for the peasants' army, for King Francesco's army!"

He laughed, Carmine Spaziante, with a deep laughter, down in his throat, the way suited to a man like him, taciturn by nature and made gloomy by life's vicissitudes. In those early days, he seldom spoke to the men. But then a hidden strength, a new violence, began to transform him, making his gestures more resolute and giving his speech a self-assured boldness. He took to calling roll every morning. On that occasion, he sometimes wished everybody good morning—as he used to say—with one of those short but resonant phrases that came to him only at daybreak, when his mind was rested.

"My good friends"—he would say—"bread does not have wings, we must move to go get it. And this year the harvest has to ripen for everyone. Or for no one."

The men were taciturn and gloomy as he was, used as they were to the mountains' silence and the inarticulate voices of the animals. They listened to him beating the guns' butts on the ground. On many faces, you could read a sort of astonishment, as of people who have not yet fully comprehended what has happened to them. This was the topic of Carmine's grievances with Cosimo: "They are people who pick up a gun to go hunting for animals, not to hunt for men."

Meanwhile the Bourbons' plotting had regained strength and the Committees flourished, so much so that in some areas they soon became true shadow-governments. Their members had to be sworn in, and the president received a diploma printed in Rome. The Committees were the ones that issued patents to the bands'

40

leaders, honorific titles, and buttons imprinted with a crown, a hand holding a dagger, and the motto: *Fac et spera*. The peasants, who could not read, thought that it was a spell against modern guns: against the precise shots of the "garibaldesi," as they called them as an insult, and against those of King Vittorio's soldiers.

The inhabitants of villages and towns, all the while, lived as if under siege; in the fields there were more people armed to protect their property than laborers, and the carts rolled without making any sound along the main road because the drivers, as a precaution, had started taking off the bells from the horses' bridles.

Antonia continued caring for me until I was again able to stand on my own. An intimacy had developed between us that had to do with the food and the needs of my body, but also flowed from her hands that were never tired, and touched me, comforted me, and made less disagreeable the dull heaviness of my flesh. Later, I thought back on her calm, on that tranquil and loving acceptance of me, and I could not explain it. Had a sudden compassion impelled her toward me at once, or was that simply her nature, obedient and helpful, but also unwary, obstinate, and adventurous?

Through her I again made contact with the world. The intermediary of her luminous and swift body was necessary to me. I had to overcome not only my physical feebleness, but the weight of my thoughts. They were a ballast that encumbered me, held me fast, chained to that bed so that I would sink down into nightmares and the slimy mire of my remembrances.

From the mountains' summits was still coming now and then a cold wind, and in the farm's kitchen someone would light the fire. Antonia, bundled in her shawl like a little old woman, endeavoured to prepare a warm meal. Her heavy gold earrings reddened the lobes of her ears, and she touched them now and then, with the anxiety of someone who wishes to be reassured about the indubitable truth of some event.

"They are a gift from Carmine"—she would say, and Carmine's name recurred in all her talks. "My mother sent me to bring him warm bread and ricotta....." She smiled lowering her eyes. "And she lost in that way her daughter and her basket." She was a very poor peasant, was her mother. As for her father, she had never known him, indeed did not even know who he was, and when she was a little girl, she confided, the little boys did not let her be; they hunted her with that insult, "bastard," that was always ready to leave their lips like spit.

Presently she would say: "He treats me like a queen," straightening herself with a naively proud movement of her head, and the shawl would slip down uncovering her shoulders. She would raise her eyelids, and her eyes would again sparkle. "Like a queen," she would repeat, touching her earrings that reddened her small, soft earlobes. And through her blushes and her smiles I suddenly glimpsed in Carmine a man I had never seen.

* *

I had fled in my nightgown and a cape, and they were now all that I possessed as clothing. Better that way. I did not want to have my steps encumbered any more by skirts and surcoats. Hands free and a bold step, that was the way I fancied myself to be from that moment on.

When I asked Antonia to procure me man's clothing, she acquiesced. I was not alone in adopting that attire, and to know it reassured me. In the disruption of so many lives, in that desperate flight into the heart of the mountains, that was a necessity to which many women had bent. "It's the right clothing," and Antonia automatically pulled with spontaneous grace her shawl that crossed over her young and strong breast. "It's the right clothing for this cursed life. It will look well on you, donna Margherita."

Maria Orsola Cardona, whom they called "la Bizzarra," was the one who procured what was needed, and that is how I became acquainted with her.

I knew that there were several women at the estate, in that period. They left faraway villages, and walked miles and miles on foot to see their husbands, or their sons. Upon arriving they would move around the rooms ill at ease, feeling their way, wary like domestic animals that explore an unknown and therefore treacherous space. Some of them preferred to do their cooking outside rather than in the ample, alien kitchen, with its oven built for rich and elaborate meals, and its unfamiliar closets that hid a great array of pottery and objects of every kind. In one corner, as it was customary in all wealthy homes, there was the deep and narrow well of the latrine. The majority of those women came and went, never stopping for very long. Some came to join the men whenever they moved and established their quarters, and remained to do the washing and cooking until the next move. But one and one only, Maria Orsola Cardona, la Bizzarra, was really a member of the band.

No one knew for certain her story. They only knew that she had taken part in the uprising of a small mountain village, Topiano, during the previous winter. She had joined a former corporal of the Bourbons' army and his group, but winter and king Vittorio's soldiers had succeeded in dispersing that handful of stragglers. Now she moved around the farm in man's clothing, with two revolvers in her belt, and she participated in all the forays. She did not have relatives or friends in the band. When I saw her, she seemed to me ugly and ungraceful, but it was the first time I faced a woman in trousers and fustian jacket. She had around her neck a rosary and a thin string from which hanged a leather pouch containing small lumps of earth that the Virgin had trod on one of her many apparitions. Her eyes, however, were beautiful, deep black and languorous, surprising in their contrast with her entire demeanor. She had long thick lashes that grew to the end of her lids making her eyes appear even longer and slightly almond-shaped. The men did go after her, even though she kept them at a distance.

La Bizzarra came and planted herself before me. She slowly looked me up and down, and went away without uttering a word. Presently she came back with an armful of clothes that she let fall on the bed cover. "Everything is here,"—she said—"all that you need, except for arms. Carmine Spaziante hands out those."

I dressed slowly. Each item of clothing required long movements; I was not accustomed to dressing without help and without a mirror. With a wide red sash I tightened my trousers on my waist; they were of a passé style, tight on the leg, and barely reached to my calf. My breast became lost in the large white shirt, and disappeared completely under the bright short jacket. Then I braided my hair again, and hid it under a cone-shaped cap adorned with ribbons. With each garment I was entering into a new dimension and time. In truth, I was not taking a new habit, but taking up a new life. Of my own will, I renounced even the last appearance of feminine propriety.

La Bizzarra was there, leaning with her back on the wall. Antonia also, seated on the bed, her hands tight in her lap, watched me with animation as before the preparations for a festivity. Other women whom I was seeing for the first time looked in through the doorway. My difficulties with laces and ribbons put now and then a mischievous glint of pleasure in their glances. But I did not ask for help.

In a similar setting I had put on my wedding gown, under attentive but concerned glances; I was helped then by solicitous hands that slipped the dress on, and tied, and pulled. Still, being agitated and clumsy, I had torn it, with a long irreparable tear. Filomena had instantly exorcised that omen by bringing together the two edges.

At last I pulled the remaining laces. I felt a curious sensation with my trousers tight on my hips and my hair completely hidden under a cap. But after all, that was only a mask to help me deceive my fate; it was but a reassuring game.

"The shirt belongs to your brother, donna Margherita," Antonia told me, and I felt the caress of the cotton, cool to my skin. "Yes, we have the same frame." I was glad not to be able to see myself in a mirror, as if a mirror could fix and confirm my betrayal. It felt like I had robbed him, together with his shirt, of a part of his manly soul and youthful strength.

*   *

On one of those evenings that were still cool but tempered by the warmth of the fireplace, Master Caronte arrived, with his drum slung over his shoulder. I had known that old man since forever; he earned his living singing announcements and banns on village streets, and between rounds he sat before his house weaving baskets. He did woman's work, but no one was surprised any more when Master Caronte sat in the sun, warming his arthritic hands with the rhythmic movement of his fingers. He sat before the house door as the women did, but unlike the women he faced the street.

His singsong voice entered the houses since time immemorial, the warm kitchens, the intimacy of the bedrooms. The drum roll accompanied the old man's steps, echoed in the courtyards and the alleys, with a long echo that widened and widened in concentrical circles, magic circles in which he enclosed the entire village with all its people. But the burghers or the town authorities paid him to say only and exclusively what they wished. They were people deprived of all imagination. Their laconic announcements bothered Master Caronte who, when he could do so without risking, added something of his own to them, maybe just a drum beat that broke up the phrase and left the listeners disconcerted. Then in the summer evenings, when there was a festivity, he turned into a storyteller, the most requested and most famous storyteller of the entire province. He liked to recount old and new village events as if they were fables, as if another sort of people had lived then in a world that the bittersweet sound of the jaw's harp made seem remote. In the winter, my father had him come into the house to warm up by the brazier or the fireplace, and I coaxed him to tell, just for me, long stories to which his sharp and cadenced voice gave rhythm and meaning. As he modulated the stanzas, he stretched his hands toward the fire, but did not look at me.

He did look at me when we met as soon as he arrived at the farm, with a new and open look. Now he could know me and recognize me, at last I deserved his acknowledgement; I deserved to enter into his stories. His observing me did not displease me; his eyes were curious but not hostile, and they were not distrustful either as were instead those of the greater part of the people at the farm. It was with Master Caronte and la Bizzarra that I found myself the day of my baptism of fire.

We had accompanied one of the women to the village, in order to collect provisions and fresh clothes along the way. As we were returning, we almost had an encounter with some *carabinieri* from the Acerro station, who were lying in wait on the main road. They saw us and they pursued us deep into the woods, firing into our group. But they were on foot as we were, and that saved us, which I did not realize at first. I heard the sound of the shots, and I felt nothing, not even the shadow of fear. It seemed that I had acquired in one moment a new lucidity, in my mind but also in my body. Never had I felt so agile and light, with all my senses awakened and tensed by an alertness that was sharp but natural, requiring no apparent effort. Behind me was the cautious stepping of Master Caronte, while la Bizzarra guided us both, opening the way in the underbrush. When she was sure that we had made them lose our traces, she stopped.

I had never seen those places. They were sad and desolate. A muddy, opaque stream ran down the valley, as yellow as the mire that opened further ahead, baring a side of the mountain. At that point the woods suddenly retreated and the marshes advanced like a sickness, a leprosy that consumed the trees and opened sores in the ground. At the edge of the woods, on our side of the river, there was a minuscule cluster of a few houses. When we approached, the village turned out to be deserted and the walls blackened by the flames of a recent fire, set perhaps by our very attackers. A thick and dense fog was rising from the muddy ground and the stream; it caught up with us, and enveloped us.

I had the impression that I was moving in one of Master Caronte's stories. Or perhaps we had truly reached the dark waters of the river of death. When suddenly, from the bosom of the village a cry rose, or a lament. We remained still, waiting. The lament was repeated farther away, under the trees. "A lost soul," said la Bizzarra, and shivered. Only then did I realize that I was trembling and that I was not able to control my trembling any more.

May 1861

The sanctuary was far from all inhabited centers and clung to the flanks of a mountain gorge. One climbed up there on foot. Mules and horses waited down below, at the crossroads, where the watering trough and the market were, and where a tabernacle of blue ceramic foretold the splendors of the naves and the magnificence of the altars. It was up there that the festivities of the Madonna of the Chain were celebrated, in the fullness of spring.

Every year, the night before the first day of the celebrations, Filomena and I went on pilgrimage up to the top of the mountain. We left at dark, when dawn was still to come, and sleepiness wrapped us in discomfort as a cold cape. We met other solitary shapes along the path, with whom we exchanged mute gestures of greeting.

The place where it was customary for us to pause dominated the entire valley, and I waited there for sunrise, over and over again with unspoiled emotions. Sleepiness and discomfort evaporated as the sky seemed to breathe infinitely expanding, and the black invisible abyss below us slowly opened up like a curtain, revealing the woods all dewy and drenched in light. I was witnessing the creation of the world. A tumultuous and ill-defined want invaded me then, of something, anything, the yearning to escape a fate already sealed, and tear open by force the wall that enclosed my life. I would then begin to plan joining Cosimo in the city, and I imagined dining in one of those inns filled with smoke and students, where one could quench one's hunger with pizzas, chestnuts, and olives. In the evenings, I would stroll the deserted and dark streets, in the company of a flock of friends, carrying the little lamp required in the city, with no aim or time watching, for the night is not measured in hours.

Later in the day the sun started burning, and the countryside would come to life. The celebration widened around us. Three days lasted the luminaries and the penances. But under the arches of the sanctuary the eyes of young women and young men met; dreams soared against that backdrop of rich silks, sumptuous damasks and brocades, and the splendor of gold and velvets. I also searched for a

47

special glance among all the glances that in turn searched mine, but I could not keep the memory of even one face, even one smile. and my imagination burned in vain.

*　　*

That year everything began as usual. It seemed that the festivities should triumph as always, stronger than war, stronger than any calamity, more alive than any man's life. And yet, that was an unusual and special year for everyone: for me, who did not have news even of Filomena, and for the men, who waited at the farm for Carmine Spaziante's orders, instead of being at work in the fields, or standing in line before the barber's shop to prepare for the holiday in a fitting manner.

Precisely in those days the authorities had revoked the right to plant and graze on public lands in the commune of Grottaperciata, which was located not far from the estate where we were camping. The revocation was supposed to be a prelude to an imminent apportionment. But the final destination of the lots was uncertain; no one knew to whom they would be assigned. Perhaps they would go to the men of substance who had already appropriated and enclosed a great portion of the property. Meanwhile, the animals had no place to go to eat.

Since time immemorial the villagers of Grottaperciata and the small villages nearby had enjoyed the right to gather wood, draw water, graze, and camp overnight on public lands. Now it was as if they had gone back to 1848, when the people of Grottaperciata had to occupy the land in order to claim their right to the use of it. A hundred of them had been arrested by the Bourbons' gendarmes, but Ferdinand II had granted them grace because he had believed them to be "more wretched than criminal." And the populace of those mountains still remembered the sovereign's act of clemency, and the impotent rage of the men of substance. But now, what was he going to do, that faraway and foreign king, the Piedmontese king, on whose side would he be? In the meantime he starved the animals, and with the animals the people.

So, after all, notwithstanding all the solemn preparations, there was no time for the festivities that year. Everything happened on the same day when a procession of men left the sanctuary itself in

48

order to go occupy the land. They were many, and all carried an olive branch, not as a sign of peace but as a reminder of the ancient rights which the community had, including the right to cut wood as needed. At the head of the procession, ignoring all caution, there were about a hundred women with crosses and white banners they had prepared in secret and now unfurled as if to defy fate. They sang litanies, dancing all the while and crying from time to time: "Long live Mary, down with Vittorio!"

The trodden dust rose thick, hiding people and beasts, so thick that at one point all one could see was a great white cloud that advanced like a storm through the countryside. Once in a while a figure emerged and the following instant it was sucked in again by the maelstrom. The wind carried intermittent voices and calls in waves. But even when the wind was quiet one could hear clearly the shrill voices of the women who ran after their children.

And above everything there was the roll of Master Caronte's drum. No one among us had seen him leave the farm, but for certain we all heard him that day. His old hands deformed by illness had found again their old vigor, and they beat an impetuous, bold rhythm, a war song.

* *

News ran swiftly in those times, carried by the anxiety of entire populations, families who had all their men in hiding. Rumors ran faster than our horses. That is how we learned that the National Guard had reached the disputed land and surrounded the terrain occupied by the peasants and the shepherds, while a cavalry squadron galloped toward that same location. The town was under siege, soldiers could be seen everywhere, and even the estate was not a safe shelter any more, and it should be abandoned. The time had come.

Planted in the middle of the courtyard, with an imposing presence and the voice of authority, Carmine was giving orders to the band, dividing the men, and fixing the meeting point. He used few and precise words, self-assured and calm, as if he had never done anything else in his life. I felt an immense and surprised admiration for that self-possessed man who was able to organize time and actions, and bend everything, even the unforeseen, to his own specific and coherent designs.

The sudden acceleration of the events began to stir me, too. I stood near Carmine, ready to execute orders that were not coming. Paralyzed by my own excitement, I stared at that foreign yet familiar face. As long as I stayed near him, in the open light of the courtyard, fear was a thin, impalpable film of dust that could be easily blown away. But I did not have the courage to re-enter the room where I had slept all those long days, and where I now felt I had exhausted experiences and efforts too great even to be merely brought to mind. Inside that room, I might perhaps come against the ghost of my own insomnias, and that would have sufficed to bring into the open my vague malaise, that insistent distress that was still pulsating under the fragile skin of my excitement, like the worm that moves slowly in transparency under the skin of an apple. And yet, I had to return inside to gather the few things I might find of use, and I could not linger any more.

Most of the women were preparing to quit the farm and leave the men. They hurriedly sewed holy relics and amulets in the hems of the men's coats, that they might be protected against the soldiers' gunshots. Each one of them was preoccupied with her own particular separation, and yet one could sense an increased intimacy in their group. In that circumstance they all felt—and so did I—that we were bound not just to one man but to a shared fate. They helped each other, handed each other small items, bread, clothing. I was still lingering as I observed all that swift activity from outside the threshold. Sweat made my shirt and trousers stick to my skin, impeding my movements worse than a corset. Any movement cost me a great effort, I could not recover the nimbleness of my limbs, and I felt as if my legs were engorged to bursting with blood in those excessively tight trousers that seemed suddenly extraneous to my body.

In the kitchen, Antonia was gathering foodstuffs in large cotton kerchiefs that she tied at the four corners with measured gestures made quick by long practice. I saw her stop, perplexed, before a tub where she had been rinsing some wash. Indecision drew small lines between her eyebrows that were blond like her braids, which she had coiled on top of her head, and like the sparks that made

50

joyous and lovely her eyes. "Well"—she declared aloud—"if I cannot take these wet things with me, I will not leave them here to mold, either." She went out with a firm step, the tub against her hip, and her round arms shining with water and bleach. She started spreading the wash on the bushes around the house, raising her arms, shaking and spreading with meticulous movements but rapidly for fear of being interrupted at any moment. The scene was so absurd that I burst into laughter. With the wash dripping in her hands, she turned around ready to hurl an insult, but when she realized that it was I, surprise stopped her short. She had not heard me laugh, ever, and perhaps—who knows—she had decided that I was born that way, with a natural impediment to laughter and happiness.

*   *

While the main body of the band moved deeper in the woods to reach a more protected and safer place, I rode with Carmine and a few others toward the occupied public lands. I turned for a moment with my hand on the saddle to throw a last glance on the farmhouse. It had the appearance of a fortress, with its massive structure solidly bound to the land by deep roots, like a centuries-old oak.

The horses, still fresh, moved with agility, not tired by the terrain. I let myself be transported by that sensation of lightness and by the breath of a current wind. I rode in the style of men, happy that my trousers allowed me to do so. At first this fact, which was new for me, occupied all my attention; then little by little a different sensation took over, which was suggested by the guarded advancing of my companions, and the caution of each of their movements. For the first time I detected with clarity the sensation of danger. I saw it in the tense faces of the men, in their manner of riding, in their silence, their pauses, and the nervous spurts of galloping. I sensed it also inside me, an elusive feeling that was not simple fear. It was a spasmodic, intolerable state of expectation. It was a wish to cause the events to precipitate in order to be, at last, beyond them, beyond waiting, beyond the anguish of waiting. Then Carmine dashed ahead in a burst of galloping and we followed. The earth raised by the horses' hooves flew into my eyes and burned my face. My life, in that moment, depended entirely on Carmine

Spaziante, his intuition and his decisions. What would we find at the end of our riding? Panic made my heart sink at every manoeuvre, every pause, and every acceleration. Suddenly I hated my impotence, and I hated Carmine Spaziante. I was not afraid of the soldiers' bayonets, if that was what awaited us at the end of the trail, and Carmine, certainly, was guiding us following a prudent design of his own. But I wanted to understand, I wanted to know. Then I thought: Yes, this is war. And this is what a simple soldier, the foot soldier, experiences, while running right and left pushed by the sharp commands of his officer, capable of moving only because of his terror to be shot from the back. Not to understand where one's life is going, that is what war is.

Cosimo's horse came alongside mine. My brother moved as if he did not sense danger, he rode without respecting the order of march, indifferent to Carmine's curses, and careful instead of helping me in the difficult points. From his expression I understood that he did not dislike such a task. He had noticed my lack of confidence and the difficulty I still had in controlling the horse, and perhaps he deluded himself that he was finding anew, through his concern, my old sisterly docility, re-establishing in that manner the order of things between us.

All the while, the woods exhibited the signs of an invasion and a battle. The trunks were splintered, hit by the guns' bullets, the grass was trampled and torn, and the roots of the shrubs had been exposed by a hail of fatal force. The dry earth of the trail was dug and tortured by the fire of the encounter. All the more singular appeared to be, in the middle of such upheaval, the total absence of human traces. The blood itself that stained here and there the earth of the trail or the ancient tree trunks seemed to have spurted directly from the earth's womb, a night discharge; and all around there was that obsessive silence, as if the woods had suffocated every breath and suspended all manifestations of life. We had entered a malignant and bewitched space; the regular beat of our horses' hooves were the distant knocking of reality on the doors of a dreamworld.

Then, behind a bush, I saw a conical hat that seemed to have been set aside by a diligent and devoted wife, ready to be worn; and then—all at once—bundles of rags scattered everywhere, broken

52

weapons, the carcass of a mule covered with flies that buzzed, inebriated, with a deafening loudness. Carmine looked intently at every bush and every rock, reconstructing the events, guessing from imperceptible signs what had been carried out in that space. He interrogated the terrain, drew conclusions from the silence of the animals, and consulted in a low voice with Cosimo and the other men. He inhaled the burnt smell of gunsmoke in the air. After that, he turned his horse around.

* *

The day was overcast, and the flaccid, suffocating belly of the clouds weighed on the earth and the woods where nothing stirred. When clearings appeared suddenly under the horses' hooves, the round eye of the sky struck me like a livid premonition. Daylight never ended. The horses dragged it along with them in their tired galloping. The men's faces enclosed in their thick beards looked deeply familiar to me as we labored together. I knew each one of them, by now. Sergeant Motta, the son of a shepherd and a weaver, whom Carmine had promoted to that rank, had been a simple soldier in the Bourbons' army. The young Gaetano Lacava, a day laborer, illiterate and superstitious, was said to charge his gun with rosary beads; he wore his hair long, divided in two bands that covered his ears, then pulled it back and tied it in a long braid. Gennaro Iannarelli was a private driver who had set fire to the coaches of the public transport that had been his torment and ruin. Last, there was Vincenzo De Leo, a daily laborer, accustomed to migrating with his family every year into the Papal States, and returning from there with a few coins, burning with malignant fevers. He used to descend toward the lands of the Church with the other mountaineers, ordered in bands; they returned together to winter on the mountains. That year they had found the border closed, and no hope for work. Instead of recruiters sent by the landowners with the deposit money, they had found Carmine Spaziante or other band leaders, who had engaged them.

We were approaching the village; the trail was smoother, the fields were tilled, and the drywalls divided the plots of land with ample and lazy coils like ancient serpents. But no voice rose from the deserted fields. An eerie silence still accompanied us. Only far away in the distance could we hear a slow and stifled sound. At first I did not pay attention to it, as if it was a part of the natural order, in keeping with that dreary day. Then a sense of alarm made me more alert and attentive. The tolling of a bell announcing death reached me.

At a turn in the road, by now very near the village, we saw a house the color of stone on top of a small bare summit. An old woman entirely wrapped in a black shawl sat before the poor dwelling. Her face was turned toward the village, whose roofs we glimpsed behind the trees a little space further. Her hands were abandoned in her lap, the palms open upward. When we called to her, she did not answer. She had the rigidity of a statue, and in her traits was the power of those ancient sculptures that sit guarding the holy ground of cemeteries.

The main church rose at the very center of the village and overlooked a large square that was set a little above the road. Shaded by three ancient oaks, the square was bounded on two sides by a wrought iron fence bordered by long stone benches.

I saw them at once, in the middle of the square, piled on the bare earth in a confused mass.

We handed the horses to a young man who had met us and escorted us to that point. We approached the scene that became more detailed: ten, perhaps more, human bodies were thrown there like carcasses, some naked, completely denuded of their clothing, their wounds exposed to the sky that was darkening in the imminence of nightfall. Above them there was the raucous and excited cries of birds, and the continuous tolling of the bells beat directly on the heart, precise and sharp as a hammer striking. The sickly sweet smell of death was beginning to spread in the streets. The villagers were all outside, a silent procession moved from the houses with their shut and hostile windows, toward the main church. Clusters of men with heads uncovered and veiled women stopped on the sides of the square to look at that spectacle of death intended by King Emmanuel's soldiers as a warning. To leave the executed men unburied: those were the orders.

The ten had been chosen by lots from among the peasants captured after the encounter on the occupied public lands. Some were strangers, and no one knew them. After an improvised war tribunal

54

came the death sentence. Having pronounced the sentence, the officers of the Italian army who were on that Council, which was formed blindly and in a hurry, retired in order not to grant the *cafoni* the honor of their presence to the execution. Hands bound behind their backs, the peasants had been led to the church-square. The soldiers pushed them with their bayonets in order to make them walk faster. A long and furious volley, and they had fallen one over the other. They had not even had the time to shout a name— their own or that of their village—so that someone could take it back to the women who were waiting for them. A name was very likely the only thing those *cafoni* had owned in their lives, and the guns of King Vittorio had deprived them even of that lonely distinguishing sign.

An orderly and mute crowd by now surrounded the square. No one dared to pray. The old women moved their lips without making any sound and raised their arms to the sky in a gesture of utter despair. We mixed with the crowd, forgetting all danger, and could not avert our eyes from that spectacle. Among the executed, I recognized Master Caronte, in his crier uniform, the drum's strap still around his neck. He was thrown in the middle of all the other bodies, precisely at the center, as if he were holding forth and all closed around him to hear an announcement or listen to a story.

I was looking with the eyes of somebody intoxicated or transported suddenly into the midst of a nightmare. In order to wake up I passed my hand over my face, my rough jacket, and my trousers; it felt as if I was touching someone else, someone alien.

Little by little I began distinguishing people and faces in that tangle of bodies. In the light breeze that had arisen after the oppressing sultriness of the day, the straight dark hair of a young man moved imperceptibly, as if to stir the implacable fixity of the face with its cautious, gentle touch. That was not death; it was much more. A dog came out of the group of spectators and slowly, with circumspect moves, crossed the square. It looked at us askance with bloodshot eyes, and the smell of death made it drool. When it reached close to a corpse, a woman set to screaming; someone threw a stone, and the dog ran away snarling. In a house nearby a funeral lamentation started. A few women, outside, began to pray and a few men answered. The dreary incantation was broken. But no one yet dared to climb the steps leading to the place of execution. Not for fear of the soldiers, who were far away by then. No one wanted to profane that altar and put an end to the sacrifice.

A young woman undid her chestnut brown braids and initiated the keening. She tore her hair by whole locks, and with her arm extended and fingers open let them fall all around the square like shining rivulets of tears dispersed at once by the wind. Red blood began to run down her face. A young girl climbed the steps barefoot and gathered from the church square a few stones stained with clotted blood. She then descended slowly carrying the stones on her open hands, and offered them to some women who placed them in their breasts, while the tolling of the bells continued falling from up high onto the small crowd gathered there.

When we moved away as a group, all together, there was no face that turned to look at us, or person who appeared to notice us. Behind the municipal building a few men of substance were waiting for us. Carmine drew them aside and for a while, all alone, confabulated with them in a low and excited voice. Clearly, the men were frightened and insisted on going inside a nearby house whose door was discreetly ajar. But Carmine returned, mounted his horse, and we traversed the village again at a gallop, in a compact formation, and soon disappeared beyond the hills.

Now began for us a wandering life. We moved without cease from woods to woods, from one mountain to another, crossing valleys and rivers, fields and marshes. We had no rest. One day we hunted and the next we were hunted. I rode up in the darkness on the loose gravel along rivers that covered the night noises with their raucous streams falling between stones and ravines. Before me was the outline of la Bizzarra's silhouette. Her hair came undone thicker that the horse's mane on her masculine jacket. She looked like a legendary animal borne by night itself in a painful dream.

The band comprised now a thousand and more members. To guide and control it was a difficult and complex task. In this task Carmine truly exhibited all his gifts. He was not the same man, the energetic but clumsy and bashful peasant I had known, whom I thought I remembered so well.

Carmine had been a good bailiff, although with rather too bold a temperament. It was precisely because of that, however, that my father had offered him the coveted position of bailiff on one of his richest properties; he had preferred Carmine, even though in those days he was still very young, to men with greater age and experience. Later he had lent him the two hundred ducats he needed to be exempted from the military service. Thus, Carmine Spaziante had never been a soldier. He boasted about it. "I never served under any flag"—he proclaimed proudly—"and I can defeat career officers."

Soon after, he married. I barely remembered the timid peasant girl who brought him in the fields a basket with bread and wine and then disappeared with circumspect reserve. She did not dare to turn her eyes around her, for fear of the glances of the field hands, and she did not dare even to look at her husband, as if it were something unseemly. She did not work in the fields with her sisters any more, as she was used to do, but earned anyhow her good 4 cents a day carding wool at home. Nine months precisely after her wedding, a difficult childbirth carried her away. The baby had long been dead in her womb and had poisoned her blood, covering with blisters and sores her face and her entire body. With his wife's death, Carmine's blood turned bitter. He became intolerant and tyrannical, and he was involved in complicated and dangerous episodes. Lastly, he killed a man for obscure matters of honor, and went into hiding. Having been captured, he was condemned and taken to a penal colony. Without Garibaldi's revolution the doors of the prison would not have opened up for him ever again. He had hoped in an amnesty for taking part in the revolutionary movement and fighting side by side with Garibaldi's troops, but in vain. He had not been alone in nursing that hope. Several outlaws, who were still in hiding or had escaped prison, had sided with Garibaldi, and after fighting for the Italian cause had asked Garibaldi for their rehabilitation. Stories were told of offers and corruption, of thousands of ducats disbursed by former outlaws against a promise of impunity. Carmine Spaziante was given a promise of grace, or help with clandestine expatriation. In truth, he received a Turkish passport to go to Albania and then Corfu. Those were names that sounded disagreeable and mysterious to a man who knew only the mountains of his own island. No matter; he had decided to leave, when a fierce and virulent fever struck him. His wife and his baby appeared to him accusing him of wanting to leave their grave unattended. After that illness he renounced expatriation. Soon the new authorities issued an order of arrest, and once again the woods opened up before him as the sole possibility of salvation. It was then that he received enticements and promises of yet another and more powerful kind. "Be ready to support Francesco"—the messengers told him.—"Not only will you receive a reward in money, but you will have respect."

"Respect..."—he said—"There is only one way to be respected: to make people afraid."

The reactionary movement, which was kindling the flame of rebellion in some parts, became a powerful weapon in his hands.

His uncommon familiarity with my brother was marked by all those experiences, and yet, when his eyes rested on Cosimo, I still read in them the old fascination. There was a long-standing intimacy between them. When he used to work for my father, Carmine, who was already a man in appearance and actions, liked to

58

take along with him that young boy with light brown hair that curled around a face as handsome as a young woman's. He would take him to the fields, to the farm house, offer him a light young wine, and tell him never-ending stories of hunts and woods, inheritances and intrigues, interminably long meals and amorous treacheries. He, who never spoke, came alive with Cosimo, and let his imagination fly. Cosimo, for his part, taught him to write his name and surname, guiding his hand made heavy by the gun, the handling of horses, and fieldwork. At times I went with them, and in the evenings I also would drink the wine directly from the straw-covered flask. Carmine handed it to Cosimo and Cosimo handed it to me. When I was between them I felt as if I lost substance, a shadow floating over their complicitous alliance.

Much time had gone by since then, time that had changed both of them. I observed them while, seated side by side, they deliberated, decided on actions and negotiations, or simply conversed. I remembered Carmine being slow and massive. Now even his manner of walking astonished me, exhibiting as it did a brashness distinctive of young men and anyone who feels fully alive in the nimbleness of all motions and the ready reflexes of legs and muscles. A new vitality that I did not know he possessed animated his eyes and made his tongue limber. Changed, yes, they were both changed. My brother still possessed his gentle mien, somewhat dreamy. Carmine on the other hand... It was difficult for me to define with precision his transformation. Gazing at him I had the immediate and tangible certainty that he was now the one leading the game. My brother belonged to him, as the woods belonged to him, and that war, and the very souls of all those men who formed his band. I also in some manner belonged to him. This thought unsettled me and made me harsher and more insolent with him than was needed. But my insolence was ignored; I remained a weightless shadow for him, at the most I was a scar from his past. So I thought, or perhaps so I wished to believe.

Toward Antonia, instead, Carmine exhibited a desire for possession, dark and jealous, that each of his gestures and glances made manifest, in utter contrast with her cheerful lighheartedness. Antonia, unlike his first wife, was always close to him and fixed her glances insistently on him, allowing one to divine too many things. He also had in truth lost all reserve; it did not matter to him any more if he was surprised as he drew her aside and shut the door of a barn or a cabin. Antonia, even when she was with me, spoke only of Carmine. She would take my hands which, held by her plump fingers, appeared ever longer and thinner in their pallor. On and on she spoke, of that thick curly beard that covered full, strong lips, and of those powerful flanks that allowed no escape. I disliked those confidences, but Antonia kept on pressing my hands, without noticing that I became colder and recoiled withdrawing my hands. I would move away from her, feeling a vague malaise that approached resentment or a spiteful impatience. Then I would shrug my shoulders: what did I care about the courting of two peasants?

*   *

We stopped for a while on the Centocavalli estate, camping around the mansion and the peasants' homes that were at the heart of those wooded, immense lands owned by a very rich and unknown proprietor. It was rumored that he lived hidden in one of the wings of that mansion, from which he never moved; when he moved, it was always in sedan-chairs and coaches hermetically closed, surrounded and protected by zealous guards in green uniforms. No one knew his name except Carmine Spaziante. It was also rumored that in truth he was the owner of neither the houses nor the lands, which had been entrusted to him through a fictitious contract by a religious congregation or a convent suppressed by the new government; the intent being to avoid expropriation and the apportionment of the immense estate. I never discovered the truth.

Carmine turned the mansion into his headquarters, and settled there with his General Staff and his advisers. I could have remained with them, but I chose to remove myself. I had found that I feared the seduction of Antonia's love gestures, the unbridled joy of her childish laugh. And I feared the openness of desire that showed intense and profound on Carmine's face. It stayed a long time on my mind, much too long, until it left a trace on my very flesh. That was the reason why I camped in the woods with la Bizzarra and the rest of band.

The men were quickly done building a small fortified camp. They worked with alacrity and swiftness to surround the cabins with a protective barricade made of stakes, fascines,[1] earth, and stones. Hundreds of axes fell on the trees. In a few hours a crescent-shaped bulwark had been built that, in the event of an attack, would allow a better defense, or an easier retreat toward the forest or the peasant homes.

Cosimo did not like my choice and yet helped me to build a rough shelter that let in the evening breezes and the morning sun. I was going to sleep there with la Bizzarra.

Very soon our cabin filled up with medicinal herbs, mixtures, and infusions. La Bizzarra was very expert in caring for wounds and illnesses, so there was always someone waiting for her ministrations. She used all sorts of things: the milky paste of finely ground potatoes against infections, whipped oil and leaves of hawkweed to dry up wounds, and for contusions a poultice made of bran kneaded with water and vinegar. Water and vinegar were also useful to wash wounds; to heal catarrh or colds she placed on the patient's chest a cotton handkerchief filled with warm ashes. Against a general body weakness she gave a warm infusion of maidenhair in which she had dipped a red-hot piece of iron. She applied boiled leaves of wild cabbage to all wounds. All the while, as she bandaged, washed, medicated, and rubbed, she would recite over the sick or the wounded some personal exorcisms, certain enigmatic words that magnified the effects of her cure. She harbored a profound contempt, la Bizzarra did, toward the physicians who used only medicinal plants and their science in order to cure the complicated ills of the populace. "Those dog-killers"—and she would spit on the ground.—"They don't know a poor soul's needs."

She would tell how one night she had seen a lamp shining at the edge of the main road; a wayfarer, she surmised, who had been surprised by tiredness or had lost his way. Instead she found a woman alone, stretched on the ground and writhing in the pains of labor. She helped her deliver right by the side of the road, tying the umbilical cord with a thread she pulled from her dress, in the patch of light of the lamp, under a sky white with stars. "It is lucky that we women have expert hands... I know, I felt them on my own flesh." That sentence revealed a secret of her heart, but I did not dare to ask her when and

61

where she had given birth, if her child lived, and with whom, or if after nine months she had only given birth to pain.

She was a taciturn woman. We might sit side by side for hours uttering not a word, and only with brief exchanges of gestures. Perhaps silence was the medicine she offered me. It was not like Cosimo's silence that compelled me to remember wrongs and sorrows. In order to recover my brother's love I always had to traverse the menacing darkness of a silence that hid snares and pitfalls. On the contrary, la Bizzarra's silence was purely that of a person breathing next to me. I could relax my fears in those restful pauses; I could touch her strong and wide peasant hand, if I was visited by fearful ghosts.

I performed simple everyday tasks and charges with the other women, for instance drawing water at the wells in the courtyards of the peasant dwellings, which were not far from our camp. We could not draw water at the mansion; the well was sealed by a massive stone on which was sculpted the same coat of arms the guards wore on their caps. Also, there was always somebody on watch, as if something precious hid in its depths rather than simply water. The drawbridge also was always down, but the guards carefully controlled the access to it.

For several nights in a row, swarms of flying insects came to die against the branches covering our cabins. It was a fast hitting, unexpected storm, a black whirlwind that drummed like hail, thick and suffocating like sand. It would last a few hours and then retreat leaving behind a thick carpet of dead insects. With improvised brooms the women would clear the ground. I observed them intently in order to imitate them, but I found it difficult to harmonize my movements with theirs. They were used to serve, I to be served. It was a habit I found to be a hindrance for the first time in my life. Compared to them I was disarmed, a child who has yet to learn everything, even the simplest matters of life. I found it hard to adapt to my new situation and to a promiscuity that had been unknown to me. Without la Bizzarra and Antonia I would not have withstood the intense contrast with the other women.

Once having been accepted, I shared risks and dangers with the men, and that was all. Deeper emotions ran between the women, and acceptance was more difficult. It was a hard thing for me to discover that truth. I felt I was being put to the test every day, but I was not allowed to know the result of the test, as in an archane and dangerous rite. My discomfort became dread; dark subterranean rivers would infiltrate my dreams, and the dreams, dragged by the eddies of an invisible current, precipitated into nightmares. Every morning, upon waking, for a moment I would not recognize my bedding, I did not remember where I was, and panic tightened my throat. Then my eyes met the eyes of la Bizzarra, and I would hear Antonia's voice calling from afar. The obscure plots the women wove against me would dissolve, and so would dissolve all the ambiguous and bothersome jealousies.

*   *

I never met close up the enemy I had chosen for myself. Never, before my capture. Once in a while I would happen to see, far in the distance, the Italian troops struggling along under the sun, their backs laden with the weight of the knapsack we called with derision "the Piedmont." But they were soldiers nonetheless, and for *cafoni* who had gone into hiding in the woods it was not easy to confront a regular army that had artillery and was also on horseback. It was true that the horses turned out to be useless in the woods, where only we dared to venture with our mounts.

Life was not easy for the bands of peasant-oulaws. But it may have been even more diffcult for that army that called itself Italian and had to fight in its own unfamiliar and hostile country. The cruelty of King Vittorio's officers toward their own soldiers equalled the cruelty the band-leaders used with their men. An iron fist was needed to maintain discipline among soldiers who for months saw not even a pallet on the floor let alone a bed, and slept without undressing wherever they chanced to be. If they fell down exhausted after brutal marches and refused to go on, they were accused of insubordination and shot in the same manner as outlaws; or, in the best of cases, they were forced to move on again with sabre and rifle butt blows. The very land defended itself against them by striking them with pernicious fevers and typhus.

Some of those officers became famous, or rather infamous, among our populations. Captain Crema. Many still remember that name. He was indeed a peculiar man, the commander of a mobile column, who liked to use a whip of his that had an inlaid handle against the peasants unwilling to obey his orders. Once he whipped the owner of a café who had closed his shop at the Italian soldiers' arrival. Another time he whipped on the public square the mayor of a small town who had refused him permission to quarter his men in the city hall. He owned a small personal menagerie, dogs, cats, and canaries that his orderly cared for and guarded. At night, in our bivouacs, the men talked at length about those curious habits, and the figure of Captain Crema hovered behind us in the dark.

I happened to go through some villages right after he did; the signs of his passage were everywhere. In Casalciprano the soldiers had quartered in the parish church not having found a more apt location; to enter the devastated church awoke a sense of dismay and confused horror. I was astonished at such havoc because we ought to have shared at least awe and respect for God's things. But in war, enemies never have the same God.

We, the women, were exempted from night watch. It was the only privilege we could claim; otherwise, we participated in all the other activities of the band, none excepted. We would also take turns in going out to reconnoiter or to make perquisitions. To the forced inactivity of the camp I preferred the risks of such forays. Carmine accepted my presence with the same indifferent ease he accepted la Bizzarra's. Often he preceded us on horseback while we scoured the countryside inch by inch, all around the villages, and all the paths from the mule trails to the carriage road. Summer was beginning to dry up the streams. At times I would glimpse down at the bottom of stony ravines strips of dry earth, barren, with not a blade of green grass. But it seemed to be almost a hallucination because the woods and the fields around us were still in full bloom, bursting with life and colors. One morning I almost stumbled on a knot of snakes, rigid as dried sticks and inanimate even to the ensnaring stillness of their pupils. I had a premonition that something would happen soon.

We were on our way to the Serra Estania mountain, midway between the village of Conca and the woods of Acqua Forano, when we heard that a detachment of light cavalrymen with a good supply of victuals had camped in an isolated homestead. At nightime we surrounded the house waiting for the dawn to attack. It was a clear night and the obsessive chorus of crickets whirled madly under the stars that shone low, utterly close. Early morning broke. When the soldiers came out to feed the horses and prepare the rations we opened fire. Carmine Spaziante immediately ordered us to tighten the encirclement, thinking that the surprise would catch the cavalrymen unprepared; instead, we were met by a steady fusillade from the windows. The attack was not going as swiftly as we had believed. Firing continued for a long time on both sides. The sun was strong and dazzled us. The siege lasted for over eight hours under a blaze that melted our bodies and clouded our minds. In the end Carmine Spaziante, fearing that the sound of gunfire might attract the attention of some mobile unit, gave the order to drive out the soldiers by setting fire to the house. We piled straw and bundles of olive branches all around and we set fire. The fusillade stopped; quiet descended. Even the trumpet that incited the attack from the top of the dovecote fell silent. Everything unfolded with terrible slowness.

There was not a breath of wind; the flames rose little by little with a light and deceptive crackling, but sharply audible in the disquieting silence of the guns. It deafened more than the clamor of the shots. The flames still wound low around the house testing the terrain before the final assault. It was a long wait, longer than the long hours of fighting. Time dragged heavily on, and I thought of the men trapped over there. I felt my skin burn as if I, too, were menaced by the flames. Each motion, each slight gesture took place slowly in a remote space at the extreme edge of my ability and desire to understand.

Then, as the trumpet of the cavalrymen started calling again, high above the crown of fire, we heard the first screams.

I do not know what happened to me at that moment. I only know that I started shooting again, and screaming as if in madness. Inarticulate cries like those of an animal; I cried with a voice that was not mine. Somebody threw himself on me and held me by force to make me stop. It was Carmine's body that fought with mine, his arms grasped me, obliged me to return to reality, pulled me toward his chest, and held my hips against his. At that point I sharply felt a change. I forgot the fire, the trapped men, and the entire horror of the scene. Those were Carmine's hands, which had never even brushed against me before, and now touched me and held me again in a tight grasp that had forgotten its reason. As if even the last barrier had broken down between us.

*　　*

Again we moved on. Men continued joining us and swelling our ranks, spurred as they were by the passion of vengeance and the illusion of acquiring riches through pillage and blackmail. And yet now, thinking back to those days, I marvel at the breath of hope that above all animated those desperate people. Their mirage was as vague and indefinite as the fate awaiting us was certain and harsh. Perhaps each one had a secret and different dream of one's own, which one did not dare reveal to a companion or even to oneself. For certain, the summer of 1861 belonged to the *cafoni* and their violent, sad hopes.

History seemed to be turning decisively in favor of legitimism. Our band had acquired power although it lost in part its agility because of the continuous influx of recruits. Every day it was becoming more difficult to continue the wearing game of attacking and retreating, which was the fighting manouver those soldier-outlaws favored. "It's the Jesuits' tactic"— Carmine would say laughing.—"You feel the wounds but don't see the hand."

The secret Committees, in the meantime, were working everywhere to make the populace rise up and open the doors of the towns to Francesco's soldiers. Foreign troops were ready to land on Calabria's coast under the orders of a Spanish general. Such were the rumors running about. But who could evaluate their soundness? Nonetheless the facts were reassuring: money and provisions were not lacking and the estates were at our disposal on one condition, that we should eat and drink—so said the orders—but not destroy.

That was the way things went for a while. Although hiding had become a problem, the mountains still sheltered us and provided us with protection. We kept on marching and climbing, and as we climbed higher the mountains changed around us, the vegetation became more dense and the woods more majestic.

More and more often now we would move on at night and we slept during the day in the open air, or in abandoned cabins, in

66

small straw huts with slopes down to the ground, or in hollow tree trunks covered with leaves, lentisk, and broom. Lying like all the others on my goatskin, with dampness and tiredness seeping in my bones, I would go to sleep at the first light of a cool and clear mountain dawn. Those nights made me forget everything: danger, violence, and the strangeness of a war that could not be fought according to the military code of honor.

Sometimes I even imagined myself to be happy. Happy in the unsuspected vitality of my body, which had dried up, had lost all its tears and its blood, forgetting in those new exertions that it was a woman's body. I thought of nothing but the mountain, of the night that plunged down the gorges of ravines, and the stones that rolled down slopes and precipices pushed by the horse's hooves. My fears fell away from my soul and were lost forever.

My clothes had acquired the wild smell that is peculiar to the clothing of people who sleep in it. Now that I had it, that odor was not displeasing to me. I did not worry any more about the scent of my body, and less still about the coloring on my cheeks, or the curls that once adorned my forehead. I had bought from a pedlar I met by chance along my path a perfumed soap, such as are made in Naples and once made delightful the water in my bath-tub. I kept it in my bag and every time I opened it the delicate aroma of the soap escaped, light but penetrating, troubling me. I ended up by making a gift of it to Antonia. At night, I fancied that Carmine would smell on her the secret trace of my former scent.

Sometimes, however, I could not go to sleep because of excessive fatigue, and then images of death and desolation haunted me. In truth, death was our constant companion. Its funereal veil fluttered behind every tree and every cliff, and inside every house; a collective and casual death that erased in me even the memory of another death. Now and then the remembrance of a gesture, or of the inflexion of a voice, startled me; but those were rare and incongruous reactions. By that time I remembered very little of him, the man who had been my husband. The harsh life I led on the mountains turned my body to stone, and the strict discipline within the band stiffened my soul. Everything conspired to make me forget. I wanted to live a hundred years in order to forget an instant. Perhaps the fever and delirium of my first days down at the farmhouse had also exhausted every capacity I had to feel remorse; soon I would indeed be able to forget. In the meantime... To forget? Ah, what pitiful lies I was telling myself! A black toad crouching in my heart swelled and swelled to bursting, exuding a dark, clotty liquid. The dense ink of forgetfulness clouded my mind, but only lightly, with a distracted and passing touch. To forget was an obsession.

The news that the King had reconstituted a government in Rome,[2] where he had taken refuge after the surrender of the Gaeta fortress, excited the souls of all the men who had gone into hiding that summer.

In those very days the struggle for the usurped land had been rekindled with new ferocity. News came of riots and disorders against exhorbitant municipal taxes, and uprisings against the increase in the price of wheat. Every day the post courriers carried from town to town the news of clashes and ever more frequent and bloodier confrontations. Bloody were also the reprisals on one side and the other. The general Della Chiesa had issued a proclamation whereby bandits and outlaws were invited to give themselves up, but those who surrendered to the military had been executed. The urban centers were patrolled without cease by the National Guard. But while the reaction was still under control and subdued in the cities, it burst unforeseen and uncontrollable in the countryside. Facing a populace that had turned ferocious, the troops of the National Guard often gave up without firing a shot. And now Francesco II was reconstituting a government. Perhaps he was even readying to return among his people in order to place himself at the head of the insurgents and the organized bands. Was there in truth a future for a Restauration, or would the woods be the kingdom of the armed *cafoni* forever and ever?

Somebody had to go to Rome to kiss His Majesty's hand and unravel the confused bundle of events. Carmine Spaziante decided that Cosimo was to be the one. Cosimo had always hated the Bourbons but now he wore a silver plate around his neck with the King's effigy and the words: *"Franciscus II Dei gratia Rex."* That pendant was heavy on his heart—I believed—as it weighed on his chest; reality celebrated its triumph and a destiny was being fulfilled.

Cosimo was leaving, then, and I was remaining alone. Who was the man who sent him away from me, who was that Carmine Spaziante who proclaimed himself Francesco's General and head of all of us? A peasant, who would once have stood before me and Cosimo with cap in hand and lowered eyes. Now Cosimo was his adviser, his adjutant, and his secretary, but it was Carmine Spaziante who negotiated with the *signori*, who dictated the conditions for entering into negotiations, and gave the orders. At times I felt it to be an injustice, an evilness that their positions and fates had thus been turned upside down. Just thinking of it I felt my heart revolt.

Before leaving, my brother copied the itinerary and studied it carefully with Carmine; even the smallest error could be fatal to him and his mission. He committed to memory the names of the people who would help him along the way, the friendly villages, and the people who were favorable to us. He placed in a small pack whatever could serve on a long journey. The eve of his departure we met alone, he and I. By tacit accord, that evening was entirely ours; no duty or fear need take it away from us.

We walked along the trail toward the woods, slowly, pacing our steps with those of the ghosts that accompanied us; familiar ghosts that at times united us and at times separated us in that leisurely stroll where we were aware only of each other's presence. We threw glances at each other as if a more direct look could have meant prying indiscreetly into the other's emotions. His sad and frowning face pulled me back, tied me to the past. And I was obsessed by the conviction, which was perhaps absurd but nonetheless painful, that I had thrown a shadow over him because of my fate. I knew that I had acquired a new and obscure power over my brother. But his compliance, his protectiveness toward me in spite of everything, a protectiveness at once somewhat anxious and brusque, did they not hide perchance a greater fear, the fear of my madness? Suddenly his dread became mine. Was I perhaps mad as I let the present drag me thus to forget all restraint, everything I had been taught, while strange desires and fantasies crept into my heart? No, rather in the objects' fixity was madness, and letting life's inertia devour us. On those mountains I was fighting my private battle with my destiny.

When we arrived at the point where the mule-path divided and disappeared further away among the rocks of a precipice, Cosimo stopped, took my face between his hands, and turned it up. The night was so clear that one could see the path weave for a long way, white under the trees that threw on it shadows as transparent as veils. Immobile, I almost did not dare to breathe, my heart seized with the fear that he might ask questions I could not answer. I knew that a single, secret moment of my life troubled him more than all else, more than any danger or separation. But I did not want, at this encounter, to say words that would be with him in the loneliness of his journey, and which distance might alter. Emotions are felt and remembered; they may become fainter but do not change. Words are interpreted and change color with the passing of time.

His hands slackened. I felt his emotion in the trembling of his fingers that lightly touched my cheeks, lingered on my eyelids, the contour of my lips, my throat, and then along my body that trembled with his. I would have wished to feel his arms grip me tightly, as remembrances returned all the while of bygone sensations and child-hood tenderness, which I instinctively wanted to have confirmed by the presence and the body of the other. I wished for his embrace. In the tips of those fingers that caressed my body with timid hesitation I sensed the same wish and the same anxiety. We did not dare, fearing that our sadness would precipitate into a useless, inconsolable longing.

As we headed back, the whiteness of the trail disappeared in the thick of the woods and darkness enveloped us. We remained for a long while hand in hand in the warm embrace of that summer night. When the lateness of the hour forced us to take leave of each other, only then Cosimo said: "If he had offended you, you were not the one who was supposed to kill him. And you were not the one who had to pay. Why did you do me that wrong?" He moved away before I was able to answer. In any event, I had no answer to offer him.

He left, alone, at daybreak.

Notes:
[1] Bundles of wood specifically made for military defense.
[2] Rome was then part of the Vatican State.

The first town to fall in our hands was Torrearsa. The attack, swift and almost bloodless, marked the onset of a long-planned campaign, the campaign led by Carmine Spaziante, General of peasants and outlaws.

We advanced in small groups, each with its own charge. The telegraph pole planted on the tower overlooking the town was guarded by one man only; he opposed no resistance when we rushed in. It was late morning, but the streets below us wound around deserted, and the houses were barred, tight and immobile in fear of the imminent attack. Torrearsa was awaiting us fully armed. Behind the shutters of some windows sudden flashes shone, perhaps the gun barrels of the National Guard. But at the first shots a fluttering of white flags appeared on many houses; it was the agreed-upon signal that the way was clear. The village was soon in our hands and in those of the insurgents.

A long day began. The disorders lasted until close to night. A cloud of dust and smoke soon rose from the burning municipal building; the archives of the commune were piled up and burned on the square, and the body of the National Guard's Commander was thrown next to the smoking remains of the archives. Brief skirmishes erupted here and there along the streets. Carmine Spaziante was everywhere. I had the impression that I saw his beard and heard his calm and commanding voice in every place. He observed and guided while remaining outside and beyond the violent frenzy that had seized the men.

If I were to try to place in order the actions and events of that day, I would be unable to do it. Every episode took place as if by happenstance and I was not in a position to connect one to the other. Wherever I turned my eyes I saw nothing but flames and ruins, destruction and collapse. Few were the dead, but great was the impression of destruction that overwhelmed me. The men screamed for no reason, as if crazed, and moved around the streets urged on by an invincible and tireless furor. In the narrow alleyways of the town we encountered the avenging specters of hunger, humiliation, and all the fears that go hand in hand with destitution. The furious excitement of all spirits flew upward on the sumptuous wings of fire, but the thrill of their own ferocity awoke a deep terror in all the men's hearts.

A fantastic apparition came forth from near a pile of debris that lay before a wall pockmarked by hundreds of projectiles: a barefoot old man, dressed in a rough sackcloth, his long long hair stiff as ropes because of the dust and sweat of many years. It was the hermit of Serra Estania who lived and prayed in those forests, waiting for the earth's demise. Now he cursed the pride of men who were attempting to preempt God's will as to the time of the Last Judgement itself.

To move in the midst of that violence troubled me more than the blood of battle. I also went in and out of the sacked houses for no apparent reason. Whereas the others looked for gold and fell upon precious objects, I lingered before overturned chairs and tables, before opened and gutted furniture. Dizzyness caught me as I witnessed again and again the violent disruption of a daily, orderly pattern of life. A sort of exultation grew inside me at the sight of those violated and upset homes, which were at last open for anyone to see and enter. But soon the exultation gave way to a sense of astonished dismay and physical malaise, as if for a blow in the middle of my breast. And at that point, overcome by pain, I gazed at the shattered doors, the lifted floor tiles, the family papers torn and strewn on the ground; even the iron balustrades were ripped away from the balconies, the warehouses had been broken into with ax blows, the jars cracked and the barrels split, so that the wine spilled on the ground in rivulets that attempted to mix with the puddles of oil.

On a bed cover I saw dark spots of blood as after a first wedding night. A small, cruel story was told by those stains, a story of violated intimacy and broken pride that wounded me more deeply than death or any other offense.

I turned around. Carmine was at the doorway and was telling me something. He did not understand my emotion, or perhaps he misinterpreted it. He fixed the stains on the bed, then fixed me with the same commanding glance he used—but not any more—

with Antonia. I retreated and went out into the courtyard with slow steps.

In the midst of all that destruction a few cane mats resting on stakes fixed in the ground remained intact. Spread in neat order on the mats, the tomatoes kept on drying in the sun. Thrown against a corner, a watchdog, its belly burst by furious blows, was still writhing in its death throes. After a moment's hesitation I went on without finishing it off.

In the street a terrible tiredness overtook me. I wished to lie down where I was, on the ground, without taking one further step. I gazed around blindly. Colors and sounds floated together in my head in a sudden confusion of my senses. But there was no escape; it was too cold in the shade, too hot in the sun, and no place existed where I could stop. I could not communicate with the others but by gestures or shouts, as if I were speaking to the deaf, being deaf myself. The sense of an infinite, painful solitude oppressed me.

The writhing of the dog, the shattered furnishings, the blood stains on the bedcover, whirled around my mind all day, obsessively, as in a furious dance. Toward evening Carmine Spaziante decided to call his men to order and had the drums sound the assembly on the main square. All gathered around his tall and massive figure as if they were looking for absolution and comforting. Their ferocity having abated, what remained was but fright and desolation; the time of law and order had returned. Darkness caught everyone by surprise as if no one had expected even that day to come to an end.

* *

At some distance from the town, where the hills began, in an isolated position and almost hidden by the thickening trees, rose the brothel. During the day the fighting had not even come close to it. It was a world apart, which only at night opened and became visible to foreign eyes. Even then, not to all eyes. It was a country brothel, but it was frequented exclusively by men of substance; for all others it was more secret and inviolable than a cloistered convent. The madam's name was Flora of Messina, an outsider like many women who practiced prostitution in the King's lands, and who moved farther and farther away from their places of origin following dreams of great and magnificent profits.

73

That evening the men, who gathered in the comfortable and well-to-do home of the former mayor, indulged in the pleasure of ribald stories and particular experiences. The rich light of the candelabra revealed the excitement of their faces. And Flora's name immediately entered their talk, with her luxurious house and her free women (a singular mark of infamy, women's freedom). "Many, when they are old, become witches by profession"—somebody asserted.

On that occasion I was by accident the only woman present, but they paid no attention to me. I was seated to one side, beyond the circle of light of the lamps, and my embarrassment made me bend my face down and turn toward the shadows, in order to avoid those men who drew pleasure from their own stories as they told them. And yet I did not remove myself. I ought to have done it but did not. Once in a while I looked up to watch Carmine's closed and hard face. I had a premonition that the day was not ended yet; its homicidal force was what congested the men's faces and loosened the restraints on their tongues and desires. At the top of everyone's desire was Flora, with her grace and severe elegance, how different from other women in charge of brothels.

Each man added his comment: one woman was lazy, the other grasping. And then there was that Roman woman who was not satisfied with the profits she drew from her women as prostitutes. In some seasons she forced them to do as the peasant women do, to keep warm between their breasts in a very fine linen cloth some special seeds from which are born many minuscule black worms; these, once placed on the tenderest fronds of mulberry trees, build around themselves a cocoon as shiny as gold. From those cocoons thrown into vats of boiling water silk threads are drawn that are wound around a cudgel. The frequenters of the brothel had protested; that was not the appropriate apparel of prostitutes. But the owner had rather lowered her prices in order to continue using the women's breasts to keep the worms warm. The men took their pleasure while thinking about the black swarming that fermented there, between those forbidden breasts.

Those tales had excited the men's spirits and aroused their lust. Carmine, who was at first reluctant, was convinced. He sent word

74

to Fiore that she should open her house to the men of his staff. When the small party started for their new rendezvous I asked to join them. They hardly showed any surprise; that day anything seemed possible. Only Carmine Spaziante showed a flash of anger and said: "What else will the devil tell you?" But in his words I caught a hint of a dare that was almost expectant. And he allowed me to join the group of men.

The streets were dark and deserted, barely illuminated by a thin moon crescent that now and then broke through the clouds. There was on the air a sense of abandonment after the burning excitement of the day. The men walked speedily, pushed on by the urgency of their desire; death, or the expectation of death, has always been the most potent aphrodisiac.

I regretted my audacity but I could not go back; it was by now impossibile to renounce my undertaking. I hid a nervous tremor under the ample cloak I had worn in spite of the warm weather in order to escape better everyone's glances. The wind froze the sweat on my face but my blood burned right under my skin. "It is perhaps true,"—I thought—"I am possessed, Satan is driving me." Truly, I do not know what impulse or curiosity pushed me that evening toward an ambiguous adventure.

The house was dark. A square lantern protected by an iron cage barely illuminated the façade and the outline of the large entrance door; but not the thinnest blade of light escaped the window shutters. A doorman opened for us, a giant with blond thin hair clinging to his head as a transparent gauze. He carried a lantern and raised it high with an old man's trembling grasp, in order to light our way. The smell of tobacco reached to the atrium, and permated every object, descending thick and nauseating into my throat. Never had I smelled it so strong. In a niche on the staircase I saw a tabernacle. Before the sacred image that was covered by a thick black veil, burned a silver lamp in which smoldered a perfume more inebriating than incense. In the salon the lamps were numerous and their lights were multiplied by the mirrors, tall and framed in gold, that ran all around the walls. The effect was of a luminosity that stunned after the darkness of the night and the stairs.

The women were grouped in an indistinct mass of flesh and silks around a divan that occupied an entire corner of the salon. At first glance they appeared to be all alike to me: the same wealth of white flesh, the same loose curls falling on necks and shoulders, the same penetrating perfume. I glanced at them in the mirrors because I did not dare yet to face them directly. Thus I perceived only some details that dazzled and eluded me. I would then gaze anew lingering on a more vivid move or color: a breast that revealed its nakedness, a bracelet that sparkled sliding down an arm, a dress that opened showing the lace of a corset.

A sour odor of sweating bodies was now mingling with the tobacco and the perfumes. Curls damp with sweat drew dark spirals on the nape of a woman's neck, and sweat made the painted faces shine and veiled the eyes. Those dewy eyelashes and those drops that ran slowly on the humid skin revealed to me the women's fright. Their fingers gripped useless fans, handkerchiefs, long fake necklaces, and under the corsets that had come undone their breasts rose convulsively. At once I lost all my timidity and I felt transported by the naked palpitating of those trembling breasts. I wished to grasp with my hands that living white fear that fascinated me, and to thrust my fingers, my face, and all of myself into that terrorized breathing. An impulsion, a will to violence rose within me such as I had never experienced yet. I had not felt it during that entire day, nor in my days in the woods, nor when I killed the man who had been my husband. The force of that emotion rooted me in the middle of the room, immobile for a long time—or so it seemed to me. I was wrapping my cloak tighter and tighter around my body and my face. I wanted to flee and could not.

The men also seemed to have grown timid; they were not accustomed to that sort of brothel, all gold and mirrors and lace. Such wealth was comforting but intimidating. They did not know what behavior to adopt, disoriented as they were, all of a sudden. Carmine alone maintained an unnatural composure. As if he had meditated such a move for a long time, as if he had planned it at length, he pulled away from the other men and came toward me. He approached so close that his clothes touched mine. A hand, cautious but steady, pushed the cloak away from my face and tried to open it.

Flora entered at that moment. She descended the stairs that led to the upper floor, the secret realm of the alcoves. She wore a black dress buttoned up to her chin with a great hoop skirt that made her look imposing and majestic. It was like the signal of a magic wand. The salon came to life. As if in a dream I saw that some women were approaching me, their flesh was already touching mine, and I could see the dark blur of their armpits. A spasm stronger than any other coursed through me and shook me to the depths, from the nape of my neck to my tensed limbs. I retreated, caught by panic. I snatched my cloak from Carmine's hands and, running toward the stairs, I attempted to return to the darkness of the street. But someone was barring my way, her silk dress was open in front, and at her every movement her flesh shone in the faint light. I pushed the woman aside and she fell to the floor with a scream, as on my fingers that had touched her clung an impression of something warm, soft, and vaguely disgusting.

I walked for a long time through the countryside where only the rustlings and cries of animals reigned, my mind filled with sensations it could not dissemble, and many, too many confused impressions it could not contain. It was not the image of Carmine to haunt me, but the trusting smile of Antonia. Not Carmine's hands made me shiver, but the thin gold chain that nestled in Antonia's bodice between her breasts. My dismay was turning to fear, it was becoming ever more piercing, it invaded my mind and suffocated me. It was a pain that tore inside my body and opened there the wound of madness. I stopped short, and with my knife I made a deep incision on my arm. The physical pain alleviated the tension that constrained my mind. I let my blood drip thickly on the ground. A long white scar remains on my arm as a remembrance of that night, almost an embroidery, very light, incomparably lighter than the marking with which were at times branded female assassins and prostitutes.

* *

The dog days arrived. Even on the mountains the earth was dried up by the heat and scorched; once in a while fires flamed up here and there, and the wind brought us the smell of burning grasses.

We went from village to village, carried in triumph by the peasants and the poor, and received with respect and apprehension by the wealthy who were our allies. But those populations, until then fearful and patient, did not wait for the arrival of Francesco's army to rise up; often when we arrived everything had been accomplished. Crushed between rebellious populations and armed bands, the Piedmontese and the liberals surrendered or died, new councils took over the municipalities, and the prisons opened their doors. One town after the other, Espinarvo, Salandra, the Roveto….The contagion ran swiftly, the fever of revolt spread from mountain to mountain, and from town to town. The road toward the provincial capital opened up with ease before us, too easy and certain. The gates of the fortresses gave way as if by miracle, and the villages decked themselves out as if for a festivity in order to receive Carmine Spaziante, Francesco's General and leader of all the band-leaders. The mountains echoed the bell-ringing that announced the new times, the great feast of the *cafoni*. Rise up, poor people!—was the cry that welcomed us every time.

Carmine Spaziante entered the towns before everyone, riding a richly harnessed horse. The villagers would cluster around him wishing to see him, to touch him, and when not able to reach his person, they would kiss the horse, would kiss the stirrups. It was a delirium. The women accompanied us dancing to the rhythm of tambourines and throwing flowers and kisses to Carmine. "Beautiful, beautiful like the wounded Christ!" In a sudden moment of silence, an old woman raised her hand to bless him: "My son, may never a thorn wound your forehead." Religious celebrations mingled with the feast celebrating the revolt. The processions walked by the gallows. King's rule or people's rule, there are no differences: to convince the people to obey no one has yet found better arguments than blood and gallows. "There is no other justice"—Carmine Spaziante would argue—"but the point of a knife or the gun's mouth."

78

Often, however, we had barely moved on in order to reach another village or another town, and already the news spread that the army had retaken the town we had left. We seemed to be in the eye of a mad whirlwind. At times, in the more important towns, in some wealthier house, we happened to find one of those newspapers that were published in support of the reaction: "The Voice of Truth," "The Independent Gazette," "The Civilizer"....Carmine would appropriate it and order me to read aloud everything, each and every printed page. Fearing that I would skip something, he expected me to show him what I was reading as he followed with his finger every line of the printing. I felt near mine his body that tensed in the effort to comprehend, and I felt great compassion: for him, for me, and for all of us. Carmine knew, and I also knew by now, that every victory was also one more step toward the end of a dream, toward an awakening. Were those in truth victories? Nothing reassured that general without uniform, not even the spreading of the revolt. The brief life of the temporary councils that were established by the legitimists and the people's fury proved him right. "We occupy a town today,"—he would reflect—"and tomorrow it will be retaken. We will never conclude anything." Now I understood him. I thought I understood him. I would place my hand on his arm. I was not frightened of his body any more, I did not move away any more when I felt he was too close.

Meanwhile the fever of destruction had spread its contagion to every one. Army and rebels, on either side, competed in destroying. King Vittorio's soldiers cut down with their cannons the forests, our refuge; where once ancient woods hundreds of years old used to rise, we now found only stumps, uprooted trunks, pitiful shreds of trees, and burned earth still black from the fire. The *cafoni*, for their part, devastated crops and harvests, and committed gigantic slaughters of domestic animals as an affront to the wealthy and to the very idea of property. The reprisals against the liberals and the attempt to destroy systematically all their possessions were by now everyday occurrences. The unburied carcasses of hundreds and hundreds of animals rotted in the most unthinkable places, in a valley that was still green, and along the banks of rivers that were already low in water. To such extremities had by now arrived the fanatical desire for mutual annihilation. Carmine Spaziante did not approve of it; he was reluctant to waste property and to slaughter animals indiscriminately. He held in greater horror destroying than killing.

Until we reached one of my father's estates. The familiarity of the place was a punishment for me. I perspired from the emotion and my fingers that I tightened on the reins kept sliding, could not keep their hold. There, in those familiar surroundings, Carmine ended by losing his wisdom. He was not able to contain any more an ancient, never placated rancor, which was born of debts of gratitude never accepted, and trusts that time had changed and distorted. And perhaps my presence also contributed to rekindling his hate and exciting his lust for destruction. He set fire with his own hand to a mound of still green branches right before one of the many barns built around the main house. A large cloud of smoke rose, and enveloped and asphyxiated the animals locked inside. Broken bleating like human screams sounded and echoed for hours in the entire valley.

That evening we camped not far from there. The animation had subsided, and the day's fatigue weighed on the encampment. Everything bothered me that night: the radiance of the night sky, the rustlings in the fields, and the uncomfortable bedding. I had again seen in its fullness the wretchedness of my situation. And I had again seen Antonia lie down by Carmine, after so much time.

It was still dark when I awoke with a start at the noise in my dream, of hundreds of hooves that filled the night with their blind despair.

*   *

A lone gunshot fired by someone lying in wait behind a bush hit me on one hip making my horse rear. I had been imprudent; I had remained behind, alone. The wound was superficial, but it made riding tiresome and ever more slow. The village where the remainder of the band had stopped was still far. The sun was scalding. Once in a while I saw a burned-out farm house, or woods from which rose swirls of smoke. The carcass of a mare was rotting near the path, and the buzzing of the horseflies was obsessive. There was the threat of pestilence in the air.

I left the beaten path for a shortcut and reached a cabin lost in the middle of the fields, still intact but abandoned, at least apparently. Thirst tormented me and because of that I approached the building cautiously, hoping to find water. Leaning on the outside wall in full sun, a young man was seated composedly and with a certain boldness, his hand resting on the ground to support the weight of his body. His stillness suggested an unreal, queer calm. He was dressed as shepherds are wont to do, in a lambskin and bright red cloth. I called to him but he did not answer and did not even stir. I went closer and dismounted with difficulty. His blue eyes were wide open and lost in a bewildered astonishment. I put my hand on his shoulder and gently shook him. At that gesture his head rolled into his lap, cleanly cut.

The fountain was drawing almost no water. A thin rivulet ran in an underground channel and dripped outside onto some tiles. While the horse drank in the greenish mud of the stone basin, I picked a large, pointed leaf from a tree and placed it at the edge of the last tile. A trickle of sweet, fresh water began to run from the tip of the leaf. I drank of that water, blue as the young man's eyes, and from that day on, death's eyes had for me a color of pale, transparent blue with that same dreamy, pensive fixity. Death had worn for me another one of her masks.

When I reached the village the streets were empty. Only five men wearing a short satin cape on their cowls were walking in a procession reciting psalms. It was a short cortege, hooded and white robed. I stopped to let them go through. The windows and the balconies of the houses thereabout were walled-in, and loop-holes for the guns opened up in the walls, as they do in fortresses. I shivered in all that silence, which was broken only by the monotonous repetition of psalms, far away in the ever growing distance.

My wound began to hurt. It was all encrusted with dust and sweat, and blood had made my clothing stick to me. At seeing me in that state Antonia was frightened. She had me lie down on a cot and called for the bath-man, who came after a while, carrying a tub and a barrel of hot water into which she poured an infusion of rosemary that made wounds heal. It was complicated and painful to take off trousers and shirt, and to detach from my flesh the fabric that had become stiff with hardened blood and the mixture of dust and sweat. But I was already better. I liked the idea of occupying all of Antonia's time, being her only concern at that moment, and her only worry. I liked seeing her busy herself for me. Her distress assuaged mine, it calmed me, and even gave me a subtle sense of euphoria, as if for a revenge and a victory at last attained. When I felt my body unfettered, I immersed my swollen legs in the water and breathed a sigh of relief. Then I entrusted myself to the able hands of Antonia who passed on my skin a wet cloth as warm as a caress. I did not notice any more either the oppressive heat or the pain. And I did not believe my presentiments.

The long awaited hour arrived at last. We received the news that the provincial capital had risen to the cry of "Long live Francesco II" and now was awaiting Carmine Spaziante's arrival to celebrate his triumph.

We moved on at dawn, notwithstanding the woeful omens of that night. A star as red as a beating heart fell from the sky leaving a wake the color of blood, which did not pale but at the first light of day. Then what was to be a day of triumph and cheer began in a funereal mood. An informer, who the day before had driven a platoon of our men straight into the *bersaglieri*'s fire, was executed by shooting. It was the first time that a spy was shot in the public view. The execution took place before the cemetery's wall with a cluster of villagers present. Carmine Spaziante in person gave the order to fire and this also happened for the first time. As the man bent and fell, crumpling under the violence of the bullets, the men on horseback were already trotting away on the carriage road that led out of town. They all wore long black coats, almost a true uniform, which were the gift of a local landowner and his only contribution to the cause of legitimism. When we arrived in view of the city, we saw from the hillside the crowd that awaited us. Carmine Spaziante slowed for a moment his horse's trot, lending his ear to the indistinct shouting, and observing with an intent look the joyous mingling of colors and people. The black and compact mass of horsemen slowed down with him. "Only the Patron Saint is missing, otherwise everybody is there" commented Carmine with irony.

To receive us on the carriage road, right before the wide and massive arch of the main city gate, stood a committee formed by the cream of the local gentry: noblemen, wealthy landowners, and priests. Some had come on horseback and some with coaches bearing on the doors coats of arms well known in the entire region. The white flag, held with effort by an elegantly dressed young man, was not the poor rag we had seen waving in the villages that clung to rocky slopes, but rather a magnificent and heavy silk cloth with the image of the Immaculate Conception embroidered in gold. It was a banner blessed by the Pope from which miracles were expected.

Our entrance into the city was saluted by the noise of fire-crackers and bells ringing a full peal. The streets were strewn with flowers; petals of jasmin, broom, oleander, and roses covered the entire pavement with a soft and brightly colored carpet, whose perfume mingled with the acrid odor of gunpowder. From the balconies crowded with people were hanging sheets and tapestries. The women wore their richest dresses, and their white arms that leaned on windowsills and balustrades were covered with tight silk gloves.

Carmine Spaziante proceeded impassively, straight and proud on his horse. But I was near him and I could see his glances wander hesitantly over objects and people as if he did not know where to rest them. I read in that embarrassed hesitancy the profound emotion that troubled him. Next to him proceeded the leaders of the city, deployed in an ample line with the count of Lenge at their head. In the midst of all those men of substance Carmine's unkempt beard looked strange. Isolated from his men, surrounded by notables in great pomp, he appeared to me almost to be a hostage, a prey, a victim destined for sacrifice. It was the moment of his highest triumph, but in that moment I saw again in him the peasant, not the general, and not the people's leader. Other men were leading the game by now, and they were guiding the joust with the experience of an ancient mastery.

Our first halt was in the main church, which was arrayed as in the feast days, with the statue of the Patron Saint on display in all its magnificence, surrounded by the splendor of gold offerings. From a gold crown attached high in the vault fell majestic draperies with the tips of their hems pulled up before the statue and held back in elegant folds supported by halberds. At the foot of the main altar a prie-dieu covered with a rich tapestry in silk velours of an amaranth color with gold fringe had been readied for Carmine Spaziante. He knelt but maintained a proud and diffident stance, head high and back straight, all through the celebration of High Mass. We women stayed on the side in a separate group. Not all of us; those wearing male attire had been forbidden entrance and they waited outside with the bulk of the men beyond the great, wide open portal of the church. I had worn a voluminous skirt over my trousers and that allowed me to enter. On other occasions I had knelt without difficulty on the floor of poor country churches wearing my masculine garb, and no one had stopped me. But that action of mine had not been sacrilegious, or inspired by brashness or indifference. At least, I had not meant it thus. It was the very strangeness of the times that prevented the observance of established codes and changed the rules of the game. Now I had the impression that something was again undergoing a transformation: the men of the old order were again arranging, in accordance with centuries-old and immutable norms, the cards that had been disarranged by insolent hands. It was an unpleasant sensation that made me feel ill at ease, and once again I felt as uncomfortable in my masculine garb as I had been the first day I wore it. Mine was not an unease of movements or body, but of mind.

*   *

The evening shadows were already descending, heavier and more sudden in the narrow streets of the city. Almost as a conclusion to the festivities, the count of Lenge made a brief speech from the windows of his palace, while on the square below gathered a crowd of men. The salons of the palace were lit, and the silhouette of the Count, high up at the window, was clearly drawn against a halo of radiance. To his right hand was Carmine Spaziante, severe and imposing, with arms crossed on his chest. After the Count had spoken everyone lingered waiting. They were waiting for Carmine to speak, but Carmine withdrew without a word and the crowd, disappointed, dispersed at last.

The festivities seemed to have no end; at night there were dances in the open air and fireworks. The squares were illuminated by innumerable torches and the arches of the luminaries also began to shine. Thousands of variously colored oil lamps traced fantastic patterns from one side to the other of the streets. The ground resounded with the dance steps, and the music was occasionally pierced by the senseless screams of some drunken man. The city folk were celebrating, but I suspected that they did not remember any more the reason for that holiday. Before the palace of the Count, which housed the staff of our band, twenty armed men stood guard. They and all the troops received a ration of plain bread and *caciocavallo*; the officers received white bread and wine. Few men of the band mingled with the rejoicing crowds, and not simply because of Carmine Spaziante's strict orders; the men's spirits were tired even more than their bodies.

I was among the guests of the palace. I can vouchsafe that the hospitality was sumptuous. Dinner was served in the immense dining room that was ablaze with lights, silverware, and crystal; the floor of rare marble shone, and the servants wore gala livery. It was a room where King Ferdinand also had dined during one of his rare journeys through his kingdom's provinces. The Countess was as young and beautiful as the rumor had it. Her black hair, divided in the middle with a thin part, fell in compact bands on her pale cheecks, and her naked shoulders emerged from a cloud of tulle and lace. A flame of excitement shone in her eyes. Her every motion and even the soft flowing of her dress around her body betrayed her city origin and her familiarity with customs and ceremonials very different from ours. She came to the kitchen once in order to check on the preparations, but hers was a fleeting apparition. More than on the kitchen implements, her eyes lingered with mischievous curiosity on Antonia and la Bizzarra, who had seated herself near the fireplace with her legs wide apart. And when I passed by the wide open doors of the dining room, I saw that the beautiful lady of the house was sitting by Carmine Spaziante and her hand, white, thin, and covered with jewels, rested once in a while on his hand with a haughty and protective gesture and an arrogance that was very feminine and seductive. The Count spoke addressing Carmine with a deference I found excessive, using the term "don" in continuation. "Don Carmine" he kept repeating in an obsequious tone. Occasionally, certain that he would not be understood, he exchanged a phrase in French with his wife.

Carmine looked strangely melancholic and he lent a distracted ear to the Count. I knew him sufficiently well to know that he was meditating something and nursing some resentment. He fixed with a mixture of satisfaction and pain his men, who devoured the elegantly served food disregarding the silver implements set next to the exquisitely decorated plates. Their faces still bore the flame of

86

exaltation they had experienced at their triumphal entrance into the city. It was then that Carmine made a gesture of superb and unexpected pride. He disdained for himself those foods prepared with care and refinement, and asked a servant to bring him bread, cheese, five boiled eggs, and a few walnuts. With a single motion of his hand he pushed aside plates and silverware, and ostentatiously set before himself, on the snow-white lace tablecloth, that simple meal of his. The Count fell silent and the eyes of the beautiful lady became icy, having suddenly lost all their seductive fire.

*   *

We, the women, ate with the servants in the dark, cavernous kitchen, which was filled with the fragrance of the bread that had just been kneaded and was rising under a cloth. Innumerable copper pans hanged on the walls throwing sparks of dark gold. In a cauldron, pieces of lamb cooked in oil, and from the shutter-door one could check on the comings and goings around the big oven that stood outside. It was a quiet, intimate atmosphere, and I abandoned myself to those smells, those happy noises, and the complex but orderly bustling of a prosperous kitchen in which I recaptured the old flavor of home. I forgot the woods, the open air, and the sun to immerse myself again in that familiar world whose serene activities were repeated every day and brought reassurance. I was invaded by melancholy, a sweet and bitter sadness akin to unshed tears.

La Bizzarra was more taciturn than usual that evening. She had told me: "They call us brigands, and brigands we ought to remain. In the mountains, not in a palace at the rich people's table." She sat by herself on a wood bench near the fireplace with her hair darkening her face like a storm cloud and her eyes like lightning among her unkempt tresses; she had the sullen wildness of an animal captured by force. The women servants and the valets avoided walking by her and murmured with hostility: "Witch!"

But soon cheerfulness would again stir the people's spirits. The abundant food and a few glasses of wine reddened their faces and warmed up their light and incoherent talk. I had taken off the skirt I had worn over my trousers in order to enter the church and, with my hat pulled down over my eyes, I could pass for a very young man. I was made aware of that when I was offered, like a man, a glass of wine. The error tempted me and made me euphoric. Glass in hand, I approached Antonia. Antonia was very pale, with dark circles under her eyes and dull pupils that forebode a crisis. Perhaps that was due to the bejewelled hand she had seen—as I had—resting on Carmine. Or perhaps it was simply due to the physical malaise that had been consuming her from the moment she had discovered she was expecting a child. Since then, Carmine had stopped sleeping with her and avoided even touching her.

I had her drink a gulp of my wine and then chose for her some meat morsels from the pot that still simmered on the fire. My solicitude made the servants and domestics smile because they believed us to be lovers. Jokes and jests flew around the kitchen. Antonia also smiled and seemed to become animated. She liked to feel that she was at the center of attention; her naïve vanity was flattered by the invidious and complicitous glances of the other women. Little by little her face lit up with the beautiful coloring of lively rose I had not seen on her for a long time. She even told me smiling mischievously: "What amorous eyes!" But my hat dropped all of a sudden and my braids fell down on my shoulders. Antonia laughed heartily at the astonishment of the servants who did not know whether they ought to be scandalized or piqued by curiosity.

Later we were alone in a large room with a canopied bed, with the curtains open over a courtyard lit by the white beams of an invisible moon. On the bright stillness of the stones loomed the monstruous and hallucination-like shadows of the men standing guard. I closed the drapes against that spectral light, and the room appeared welcoming and pretty. It was a woman's room because on a table there was a small loom and everything needed to embroider, including a basket filled to the brim with spools of white and colored thread, crochet-hooks, and precious bodkins of bone and ivory. Antonia pulled my braids up on my head: "With short hair like this, you could really be a handsome boy to be covered with kisses." It was the first and only time she allowed herself the use of the familiar address with me. Still caught up in the vaguely unsettling excitement of that day of celebrations and playfulness, I yielded to the suggestion of her words and the allure of my imagination. I searched in the basket and, having taken hold of the scissors, I went to the mirror and cut off my hair. Once I had accomplished the deed, I spread the tresses on the bed in a gesture of mourning for an old myself and I shook my head. My head was light, oh, so light that I felt it was vanishing.

*   *

Those were the days of plenty. We ate well and we slept in elegant beds. The troops also had rich lodgings after we requisitioned the empty palaces of the gentry. Those days were few, all told, but going through them was like creeping through a subterranen passage dug inside a mountain. What did it matter that we could sleep on soft mattresses in real beds instead of pallets or the bare earth? The fire was blazing in the kitchen without interruption but the warm food brought us no comfort any more. Our forced inactivity made everyone nervous, overexcited, the women more than the men. Brawls and quarrels broke out more and more often. Meanwhile in the Count's palace the silver and the porcelains had disappeared as if by magic. The beautiful lady of the house had been escorted to a far away country home, safe from any reversal of fortune. She had left in a closed coach, a veil over her face to protect it from the sun and the dust. The Count, who remained in the palace, was more concerned with the papers concerning the public lands and the estates under contention than about the city's defense and the new city ordinances. It was rumored in the kitchens that King Vittorio was in the process of distributing the lands, but the peasants who turned out to be absent from their homes for no plausible reason would be excluded from any benefit. In some provinces the commissary in charge of the distribution was already at work and the local authorities had compiled lists of men who were absent or suspected of brigandage, so that the commissary could take that into account in the assignments.

Being among the servants I sensed with greater clarity the moods floating about me and I understood that the wind was shifting direction. But I did not understand more than that and I did not dare to make predictions. The fiery and exhausting breath of summer was blowing. If there was something that frightened me, that was Antonia's ill health. I forced her to eat, going even to the length of feeding her as she had done with me in that distant day when Cosimo had taken me to the farm house.

In the city also the atmosphere had become heavier. After the celebrations, a time of waiting had begun, and in that waiting fears and suspicions of all sorts were taking form. No more tapestries or flowers filled the streets, but dust that dried our throats, weakened our limbs, and brought pernicious fevers and illnesses. All activity was still, suspended. Only the poor who lived from day to day roamed the streets. The children still gathered dung in their baskets, which was going to fatten orchards and vineyards, but no one removed the trash and it fermented under the August sun. The smell of putrefaction was everywhere; it was a breath at times light and at times heavy, as insistent as the flight of a vulture. Legions of flies flew ferociously in the backstreets amid the desperate poverty of blind alleys run through by foul-smelling rivulets. Once in a while I would see a woman sitting before the low entrance of a hovel who heated a blanket on a brazier, a clear sign that someone in the house was ill and the August heat was not sufficient to overcome the shivering caused by fever. Children and beggars owned the streets. The women did not even dare to look out of the balconies. Few of them still went to church for mass, and then only early in the morning.

I would roam exploring the city around and around. It was the first time I was setting foot there. Cosimo, instead, was familiar with those streets, those houses, and those fountains. Cosimo's remembrance came back insistently; memories and nostalgia seeped into my mind in unexpected and distorted ways. I would find myself looking with Cosimo's eyes at the empty markets, the palaces, the monuments, and the closed shops that were still displaying cheerful signs of all colors. I crossed streets and squares with his long and bold steps, and my mutilation, that hair cut short and curling in all freedom, helped my fancies. I would shake my head to feel in all their lightness my tresses touching the nape of my neck, while the curious eyes of women shone from behind shutters and half-closed doors.

*   *

Danger was close upon us. Our informers warned us that numerous columns of soldiers had left the surrounding centers and were advancing on the capital. In the towns around us, even in the smallest ones, the liberals were gathering and organizing the National Guard. It was necessary to move out before the city turned into a deadly trap. It was difficult anyhow for us to leave the city as we had entered it, all together, in the manner of victors. The Count decided to rejoin his wife and counseled Carmine to go again into hiding. It was wise advice, but useless and obvious. The other bandleaders were already putting pressure to get out of the city and scatter into the mountains. But Carmine Spaziante, the general, hesitated. He remained ensconced in the palace while discipline was slackening in his small army, among the men who had followed him from the first into so many battles. There had been some disertions, few but enough to send a dangerous signal. La Bizzarra had long disappeared; I had not seen her since that first night after our triumphal entrance. Some asserted that she had sought refuge in a nearby village, others said that she had returned to the mountains; I was not able to ascertain which of those assertions had any truth in it.

And Carmine Spaziante still lingered, bound to that place by a spell or an enchantment that imprisoned his mind. He seemed to recoil from leaving that palace which, empty of servants and owners, looked now as a refuge of insubstantial shadows. Only an old woman had remained who reminded me of Filomena. The men standing guard at the main door were also taciturn. Caught in a superstitious dread, they did not exchange those jokes and reparties with which they once used to enliven their bivouacs.

Something troubled Carmine Spaziante, and it was not simply the difficulties and worries of the present moment. His eyes were red and sunken in their sockets as if he had not slept in a long time; his face enclosed by his unkempt beard was becoming paler and more tense with every passing hour. He paced with long strides through the halls of the palace, pushed by an avid and insatiable curiosity about every object and every thing that bore witness to a noble and magnificent past. He had me explain to him one by one the mythological scenes painted on the walls and the ceilings of the salons, the allegories, and the meaning of the events shown in the paintings. On the walls the portraits mingled pell-mell with biblical episodes or pagan myths. The noble ladies of the past century posed mostly in disguises, as gypsies, bacchants, and improbable weavers gracefully adorned. I was struck by a very beautiful sybil with hair coiled in a mass of curls, whose heart and gauzy dress had been torn by a bullet that had pierced the painting's canvas. I explained everything to him, following him from salon to salon and from corridor to corridor until we reached the chapel, small and intimate. There Carmine stopped before a painting that represented the Virgin rising to heaven while she crushed the devil in the shape of a serpent with her foot that was still on the ground. The serpent, even from under the small imperious foot, raised its head to the point of touching the divine dress spurting flames of pride.

"Such a sin of conceit! To be a *cafone* and to have ideas like a gentleman." Prodded by I do not know what association of thoughts and impressions, Carmine said: "That is how I was born, with bitterness in my heart and rebellion on my mind. And with this immoderate yearning to overcome, to want to be somebody. Even a great criminal." He looked at me with the hard, rapacious expression I had learned to recognize. Then his eyes became milder as his fingers circled my arm. "These delicate wrists should never have had to hold the weight of a revolver." As we turned back, the wound opened between the Sybil's breasts looked like a purposeful affront, as if someone had wanted to tear the heart out of fate itself.

*　　*

One morning I awoke with my mouth full of dust and my ears full of the noise of something collapsing: the wall tapestry had torn and a piece of the wall had fallen revealing the nest of a bat that started flying here and there in the room, blinded and frightened. I remained stretched on my bed looking at the tapestry in tatters and the wall with its rough hole. I also felt I was gnawed by a night animal that dug inside me with cruel and rapacious claws. It kept digging and digging to escape from my breast. Until that moment I had prevented myself from thinking and remembering, but the wings of the bat had now disturbed the evil dust of remembrance. And I was becoming poisoned.

The smoky flame of a candle that was nearing its end flickered against the mirror, and I vacillated like it from remembrance to remembrance and from memory to memory, falling every time back into the present. Mine was a desperate flight toward death, a death that would bring me nothing but shame. Was that where my adventure led me, that fancied freedom which had taken me into the mountains to fight, against my wishes, a war that was not mine? Remorse was a burning sting I was not able to pull from my flesh. The horsefly of remorse kept stinging me, but in the sore it had opened lay hidden another impossible sentiment: a profound compassion for the man I had killed, the man I had kept myself from loving. The feelings of alienation and repulsion had paled and now they had become regret, a macabre and absurd nostalgia. But were matters really thus? If I felt regret, it was in truth for all that which fate had not allowed me to possess: above all, tranquillity of mind, and then a capacity for oblivion.

The flowers I had arranged in a vase on the marble top of the dressing-table and had not replaced were now rotting, and the room smelled of dead flowers. Everything was impregnated with that odor, even Antonia's blond hair on the pillow next to mine. Antonia, who used to be so helpful and caring, so full of attentions and lovingness, she also was now indifferent to everything and everyone but the suffering of her own body. Neither my apathy nor Carmine's worried concern touched her. Or perhaps she suffered because he did not come close to her. Whatever the reason, she suffered quietly and silently. She knew that over them hovered the remembrance of that other child, the one Carmine had never seen because it could not be extracted from the mother's womb. I felt bewildered before Antonia's wordless pain and in that bewilderment I vainly wondered which of my feelings I should obey. As a crazed compass needle, I did not know any more which was my pole of attraction.

It was no longer time for lingering. The summer of the great reaction was over, and a new page was being turned. One by one small groups of men left the city. They were moving on with the firm purpose of bringing war to all established orders of society, and I became convinced that the political color of legitimism would not for very much longer inform their actions. They were again outlaws, vindicating la Bizzarra; they were again going into hiding on the mountains.

Carmine Spaziante reverted to being the able and astute leader he had always been. He divided his men in small bands and assigned to each a territory where it could operate without hindering the others. He then traced a different itinerary for each band and arranged to meet them in a town located in a far away province. From there, having reunited, we would depart together toward a common objective. However, he said, it was opportune to operate separately for a long time, avoiding to attack towns, and eluding the troops. The military rule was beginning to make itself felt. A long military rule, which was going to culminate (but no one would have imagined it in those days, as difficult as they were) in the state of siege proclaimed for the entire continental South. That was the strange and monstruous fruit of the new constitutional regime. The protections guaranteed by the statute that represented the political progress of which so many Southerners, me included, had dreamed, turned into their exact opposite, their very negation.

The men left, but Carmine Spaziante remained a while with a few others as if he wanted to postpone as long as possible the moment of flight. It was a moment that marked the end of the confused but tenacious hopes whose deep roots drew nourishment and substance from the blood and suffering of so many *cafoni*. He moved on when the soldiers were already under the city walls.

Antonia had decided to surrender to the demands of her body and find refuge, until the time of her delivery, in the home of a midwife who lived in a nearby quarter of the city. I was going to escort her and later rejoin that small band of men. As I helped her to tie her skirt a thought crossed my mind for a moment that I, and I alone from then on, would be at Carmine's side. There would be no protection by Cosimo, and no body of Antonia between my desire and his. At that thought I felt an invincible, deep seated hostility reawaken.

That is why we were the last ones to leave, and it was that brief delay to cause our perdition. By the time we went outside to go around the palace and reach the alley behind it, the soldiers had surrounded us. They opened fire; the first bullet hit Antonia in the middle of her breast. I succeeded, I do not know how, in dragging her to shelter behind the massive portal of the covered atrium that

94

led to the courtyard. Moss stained the walls, filling the atrium with the odor of ancient mold, and down the majestic stairway came a strong breath of stale cold. Antonia's blood was warmer than the useless sunbeams shining weakly in the courtyard. Her head kerchief had come undone and her hair covered her face. I freed her forehead of her disarrayed tresses and crouched on the ground holding in my lap a face that was slowly losing its color. She moved her lips trying to say something. I leaned further down holding with cautious firmness her face between my hands and looking fixedly into her clear eyes, deeper and deeper, losing myself inside her, inside her death. I remained thus feeling nothing, seeing nothing but Antonia's pallor. The blue vein on her temple was pulsating no more and had become as dark as a bruise.

When I raised my eyes, right before me on the threshold, a few paces away, a soldier was pointing his weapon and taking aim. I did not see his face with the light in back of him. I only saw his steady, tall figure and the mouth of that gun. Slowly I placed on the ground the blond head of Antonia, stood up, and with an unhesitating motion I opened my jacket displaying my breasts in the full light. The gun was lowered.

* *

Why did I refuse death? Why did I claim (and obtain) the right to live by revealing my femininity, my naked breasts? It is a question I have asked myself an infinite number of times in all these years. Was it so strong, then, my desire to continue that harsh life, tormented by sorrowful remembrances? A life without aim and without goal...except our common one, at the same time dreamlike and real. All destinies tend toward it as if toward an unconscious aspiration, a temptation none of us is able to escape.

I stood up with my hands and my lap full of Antonia's blood. It was an impulsive reaction, unmeditated and suggested more by pain than by a desire to be saved. In order to accept passively our own death we must be empty of all feelings and have gone beyond pain itself. I had instead risen under the lash of pain and I had bared my breast because I was not able to fire a weapon and react with all the violence I certainly harbored in my heart. It was impossible for me to give death but also to accept it. Perhaps...perhaps there was

95

also something more. My agony over Antonia, by itself, would not have given me that decisive and instinctive swiftness. There had to be present another impulse, a hidden and more obscure motive that incited me to postpone the final settling of all accounts.

Much later, during my trial, I learned that in the very same day, precisely at that time, my brother had died. The coincidence made me tremble, although it was news I was somehow expecting. With his death the circle of my life truly closed but I remained inside, a prisoner.

It is a strange faculty, memory is. It possesses an uncontrollable force all of its own; it chooses, independently of our will, the things to remember and those to be forgotten. At first, I had the impression that I could remember nothing of Cosimo, not even the beauty of his face. Instead, I felt vividly the sensations and emotions his presence had awakened in me ever since we were children. They were contradictory emotions, of jealousy and love, rivalry and deep understanding. I was the model sister who played and ran in the garden behind the house and in the parc, but sedately and always remaining within calling distance. He, on the other hand, disappeared and came back from mysterious excursions all torn and out of breath, his eyes bright with excitement. And I subdued my desire to run after him and discover the secret of his games so much more attractive than mine. I faked blame in order to maintain at least the superiority I was officially granted, while in truth I envied, and betrayed with my behavior, that disobedience of his, which was so happy and spontaneous.

And now he was dead, that brother of mine so envied and desired.

But what had really happened? The news I was given was discordant and brief. I was told that he had almost reached safety and had practically arrived at the border of the Pontifical States when men of the National Guard had spotted and pursued him. While jumping a ditch his horse had become lame, he had to abandon it and enter the woods to make them lose his trail. He had been found at dawn, having bled to death because of a wound by a mysterious bullet. Who had shot him? Not the National Guard who had hunted him in vain. Who had he met in the woods on that last night of his?

96

At times I have the impression that I am again envious of him, perhaps envious of his lonely death. We had parted with something unresolved between us, a question, an enigma that troubled his spirit, and the obstinate silence of mine that offended him. But how was I to tell him about a marriage that for him was natural and inevitable? How could I tell him about the swamp of desolation in which I was sinking little by little with a slowness more horrible than death?

"If he had offended you…" Cosimo had asked me. But in his question there was an assertion, a certainty. He had not been wrong. Yes, it was an offense that had guided my hand: the violence against my body. The limit had been reached, the vase had spilled over. But no offense would have given me the strength necessary to strike, and strike to death, if my despair had not grown day after day until it became hate. He had left me, Cosimo had, that long ago night with the regret of not knowing and not being able to follow me any more in the unexpected and disturbing twists of my life. There was again a challenge between us, as in one of our absurd childhood dares. But this time he had not given up; his answer was perfectly symmetrical and reestablished a balance between us. Because I will never know how my brother died, which ghost or living being interrupted his journey and put an end to the hopeless and aimless adventure we had shared.

The first days after my capture were horrible. No sooner had I been incarcerated than I was subjected to a series of medical visits. I was made to undress an infinite number of times, and they visited me probing even my intimate parts. They searched me with violent and hostile hands saying that they wanted to be certain I did not hide anything. They kept telling of a bandit brought back from France who had hidden a golden *marengo* inside a wound in his leg. I have never understood, in all sincerity, the true meaning of that procedure and the motives for such a cruel and useless violation. I cannot believe that they were meant simply to humiliate me. But if their aim was to break all remnants of resistance and pride through my body's humiliation, they did succeed. At the end, I felt shame of myself and my body. I was not able to think of anything else, I lived in the disgust of my own flesh.

But fear, no, I had no fears except one. I thought at first that they would execute me without a trial, which was a far from unusual procedure, and I was afraid that they would shoot me at night, whereas I wished to die with the sun, with its light. That fear made me cowardly and led me to sacrilege. I approached the confessional solely in order to ask the priest for that grace. But he said: "I do not have that power."

The trial was celebrated a long time after my capture. The chief prosecutor was absent and whoever replaced him temporarily did not want to take on any responsibility, not knowing if the government wished to show clemency, or on the contrary severity, toward those accused of brigandage. Later on, when the military tribunals were established and together with the army broke down all will to resistance of the *cafoni*, the issue was resolved.

I escaped, but by little, to that kind of trial. That notwithstanding, I was condemned to death. To my knowledge, I am perhaps alone among the women who participated in the mass reactionary movement of 1861 to have received so severe a punishement. Such a sad record! But mine was a clear case of ordinary criminality, as even my defense attorney, overcome by his conscience as a citizen and a patriot, had to acknowledge. In my case—he said—"the common crime had preceded the political, and then had borrowed from the latter its pretext." My penalty was however commuted to life imprisonment. After a sentence that was meant to serve as an example, such was the grace I was granted: a penitentiary for life. Should I have been grateful? I had not asked for it. I was accustomed to the idea of death, not to the idea of life imprisonment. The very trial seemed to me more painful than a quick and unmourned death. I was only spared the anguish of seeing my relatives. None of them attended the trial, and that was an immense relief for me; I would not have withstood the pain and suffering of seeing them before me, my father above all. Better to die, a thousand times better to die than to be compelled to face him. My father did not appear, ever, nor did Filomena. Filomena…how could she deny me a shadow of compassion, some human warmth? Perhaps she had been prevented from coming, or perhaps she also had died, who knows. Instead, I met immediately the looks charged with hate and contempt of my husband's family.

The day of the trial the tribunal was utterly crowded. I had been provided with woman's clothing, which I requested black, as in mourning. It was the first time in months that I was in the open air and my eyes were not able to sustain the light any more. The ample size of the locale frightened me after my long sojourn in a cell; dizzyness carried me into a state of loss of conscience and prevented me from focusing on what was around me and understanding what was happening. In the torpor brought about by the extreme weakness of my body I almost did not hear the questions and the answers of the lawyers. But there was little to hear and even less to be understood. As far as I am able to remember, the pleading of the defense was not that distinguishable from the words of the prosecution. The reasons brought by the prosecution, however, made an impression on me, and I endeavored to follow that voice agitated by eloquence.

"On the pale face of that woman"—said the accuser—"one can read the precocious depravation of her spirit. From her eye shines forth the pride of the criminal and contempt for society's laws. Her prominent cheekbone, her eye, and her livid lips are manifest signs of her immorality more so than what we learned from the written depositions and the oral testimonies."

The word of that man at last stirred me. I felt the temptation to abandon myself to his judgement and his condemnation. I wanted him to convince me also, I wished to be convinced of my guilt which I recognized no more. What crime were they accusing me of, what misdeeds was he debating with such fervor? After that, the same man, using the same tone of voice, asked me an infinite number of detailed questions to which I did not give an answer, ever. He asked me among other things if it was true that I was wont to wear masculine attire and if I did not find such habit of mine repugnant. At that moment, and only then during the entire trial, I believe I had a brief smile. The thought coursed through my mind that perhaps Joan of Arc had burned at the stake for that reason also, for having worn masculine clothes. So jealous men are of their prerogatives, even of the least among them.

When the prosecutor had terminated, I was shaken by the words of the public defenders, equally as agitated, for that seems to be the manner of showing solemnity in the courts. They spoke to me and the other women more than to the jury: "Ignorant women, you stepped on the most sacred rights of society, public peace and private property. Let all of Europe know that there is no force capable of shaking and destroying the order established by Divine Providence."

The other five accused were illiterate peasant women. The eldest was 45 years old and the youngest 15. They were astonished but respectful. I heard them give detailed and humiliating explanations for anything on which they were interrogated: their life in hiding, the origin of the jewels found in their possession, even the provenance of those humble earrings that evidently and legitimately belonged to their lives as country wives. And they would go at length into stories of rapes and abductions, and of conjugal and daughterly duties, in order to explain their participation in battles and uprisings. They were always passive, always dragged into life's vortex in spite of their own wills. Provided they saved themselves, they would deny themselves and their companions. I could understand them, but each one of their words was a blow that wounded me. I avoided looking at them in those moments; I would fix a point before me and move away from that time and that place. I attempted to do it, although it was not easy.

The courtroom was guarded by the military, and yet it was filled with people who had come from everywhere, a sea of faces, of unknown traits that became blurred before my eyes. Notwithstanding the difficulty of doing so, I was able to single out amid the crowd two women who were dressed in black like me with a heavy veil covering their faces. I had the impression that I recognized in the somewhat clumsy movements of one of them la Bizzarra. Was it a hallucination? Or perhaps an optical illusion due to the distorting veil of the tears welling in my eyes wounded by light and exhaustion? But at that moment I was pleased to fancy that it was truly la Bizzarra who had come down from the mountains for me. The two women stayed to the end.

As I was returned to my cell I heard, clear within me, the voice of la Bizzarra answering the not welcome witticisms of a band leader: " A woman outlaw, that's what I am, not the woman of an outlaw." The remembrance of those words gave me back strength and dignity.

Sometimes in my dreams I am again walking along the frescoed halls of the palace where the last fires of the reaction died and with them also the last triumphs of Carmine Spaziante, general of shepherds and *cafoni*, now serving a life sentence like me; bound to me, in the end, by the same senseless fate.

I walk across that empty palace moving from room to room in a dizzyness of perspectives, and each hall has a heavy and massive door that inexorably closes after me, preventing me from going back, pushing me in a set direction. Only one time can that palace be crossed and in one direction only.

Suddenly I realize that I am nearing the last room, I am nearing the door that closes all the doors, and at that moment I regret having gone through those places with an impatience so precipitous that I cannot remember even the colors or the lines of one image. I fear, when I wake up, that I will die like a little girl who has neither the sense nor the consciousness of her own past, having gone through the halls of the palace at a run, pulled by the impatient hand of her mother. Then, in my mind, I go back again and again visiting my past, like a dog on a chain who cannot be resigned to remain still in that limited and prescribed space.

The silence is broken only by the nearby sound of high tide as the water breaks against the walls of the penitentiary and runs down again, turning my cell to ice. Soon I will cease pursuing the echo of that long ago summer, and the rustle of my pen on the paper will also cease. I have filled the last leaf of paper. I have written the last word. And now?

Printed and bound in Canada

Bibliography

Bedani, Gino and Bruce Haddock, eds. "Introduction" 1-10 in *The Politics of Italian National Identity.* Cardiff: University of Wales Press, 2000.

Clark, Martin. *The Italian Risorgimento.* London: Longman, 1998.

Cutrufelli, Maria Rosa. *L'invenzione della donna. Miti e tecniche di uno sfruttamento.* Milan: Mazzotta, 1974.

___ *L'unità d'Italia: guerra contadina e nascita del sottosviluppo del Sud.* Verona: Bertani, 1974.

___ *Disoccupata con onore. Lavoro e condizione della donna.* Milan: Mazzotta, 1975.

___ *Operaie senza fabbrica. Inchiesta sul lavoro a domicilio.* Rome: Editori Riuniti, 1977.

___ *Le donne protagoniste nel movimento cooperativo . La questione femminile in un'organizzazione produttiva democratica.* Ed. Maria Rosa Cutrufelli. Milan: Feltrinelli, 1978.

___ *Economia e politica dei sentimenti. La "produzione" femminile.* Rome: Editori Riuniti,1980.

___ *Il cliente. Inchiesta sulla domanda di prostituzione.* Rome: Editori riuniti, 1981. Now *Il denaro in corpo.* Milan: Marco Tropea, 1996.

___ *Donna, perché piangi? La condizione femminile in Africa Nera* (Rome: Mazzotta, 1976. (*Women of Africa.* London: Zed Press, 1983)

___ *Mama Africa. Storia di donne e di utopie* (1989). Milan: Feltrinelli, 1993.

___ *La briganta.* Palermo: La Luna, 1990.

___ *Complice il dubbio.* Milan: Interno Giallo, 1992.

___ *Il pozzo segreto.* Cutrufelli, Maria Rosa ed. Florence: Giunti, 1993.

___ *Canto al deserto. Storia di Tina, soldato di mafia.* Milan: Longanesi, 1994.

___ *Nella città proibita.* Cutrufelli, Maria Rosa ed. Milan: Marco Tropea, 1997. (*In the forbidden city.* University of Chicago Press, 2000).

___ *Il paese dei figli perduti.* Milan. Marco Tropea Editore, 1999.

___ *Giorni d'acqua corrente.* Milan: Il Saggiatore, 2002.

Della Coletta, Cristina. *Plotting the Past. Metamorphoses of Historical Narrative in Modern Italian Fiction.* West Lafayette, IN: Purdue University Press, 1996.

Donne tra memoria e storia. Capobianco, Laura ed. Naples: Liguori, 1993.

Frosini, Vittorio, Francesco Renda, Leonardo Sciascia. *La mafia.* Bologna: Boni, 1970

Gendering Italian Fiction. Feminist Revisions of Italian History. Marotti, Maria Ornella and Gabriella Brooke eds. Cranbury, NJ: Fairleigh Dickinson University Press, 1999.

Gordon, Ann D., Mary Jo Buhle, and Nancy Schrom Dye. "The Problem of Women's History," in *Liberating Women's History.*

Haddock, Bruce. "State, nation and *Risorgimento*" in *The Politics of Italian National Identity.* Pages 11-49.

Heyer-Caput, Margherita. "Il concetto di 'verità' nella narrazione 'al passato' di Marta Morazzoni" *Italica* 79,1 (2002) 62-79.

ItaliAfrica. Bridging Continents and Cultures. Matteo, Sante ed. Stony Brook, NY: Forum Italicum Inc., 2001.

Jeannet, Angela M. "All'uscita dal tunnel." *Tuttestorie* 5 (June-August 2000) 20-22.

___ "Making a Story Out of History" in *Natalia Ginzburg. A Voice of the Twentieth Century.*

Lazzaro-Weis, Carol. *From Margins to Mainstream. Feminism and Fictional Modes in Italian Women's Writing 1968-1990.* Philadelphia: U Pennsylvania P, 1993.

___ "Stranger Than Life? Autobiography and Historical Fiction" in *Gendering Italian Fiction* 31-48.

Liberating Women's History. Carroll, Berenice A. ed. Urbana: University of Illinois Press, 1976.

The Literature of Fact. Fletcher, Angus ed. New York: Columbia University Press, 1976.

Literature and History. Schulze, Leonard and Walter Wetzels eds. Lanham, Md.: University Press of America, 1983.

Mack Smith, Denis. *The Making of Italy. 1796-1870.* New York: Walker and Co, 1968.

___ *Modern Italy. A Political History.* Ann Arbor: University of Michigan Press, 1997.

Manzoni, Alessandro. *On the Historical Novel* (1850). Tr. by Hanna Mitchell and Stanley Mitchell. With an introduction by Sandra Bermann. Lincoln: University of Nebraska Press, 1984.

Marotti, Maria Ornella. "Revising the Past: Feminist Historians/Historical Fictions" in *Gendering of Italian Fiction.* Pages 49-70.

Natalia Ginzburg. A Voice of the Twentieth Century. Jeannet, Angela M. and Giuliana Sanguinetti Katz eds. Toronto: University of Toronto Press, 2000.

Pantaleone, Michele. *Mafia e politica.* Turin: Einaudi, 1962.

The Politics of Italian National Identity. Cardiff: University of Wales Press, 2000.

Renda, Francesco. *Storia della Sicilia dal 1860 al 1970.* Vol. I. Palermo: Sellerio, 1984.

Romeo, Rosario. *Il Risorgimento in Sicilia.* Bari: Laterza, 1970.

Rossi, Monica. "Rethinking History: Women's Transgression in Maria Rosa Cutrufelli's *La briganta*" in *Gendering Italian History.* Pages 202-222.

Scott, Joan Wallach. *Gender and the Politics of History.* New York: Columbia University Press, 1988.

Villari, Rosario. *Il Sud nella storia d'Italia.* Bari: Laterza, 1966.

White, Hayden. "The Fictions of Factual Representation" in Angus Fletcher, ed. *The Literature of Fact.*

___ *The Content of the Form. Narrative Discourse and Historical Representation.* Baltimore: The Johns Hopkins University Press, 1987.

Maria Rosa Cutrufelli

Born in Messina (1946), Cutrufelli received her Doctorate at the university of Bologna. She began her career as a journalist, and published numerous volumes of sociological essays. In the late Seventies and early Eighties, she had her first encounter with the African continent. Two books emerged from that experience: *Donna, perché piangi? La condizione femminile in Africa Nera* (1976; translated into English as *Women of Africa*, London 1983), and *Mama Africa. Storia di donne e di utopie* (1989; reprinted, Milan, 1993).

She was founder and editor of the journal *Tuttestorie* (1990-2002). Some of its issues have become fundamental texts in women's literature: *Il pozzo segreto* (Florence, 1993); *Nella città proibita* (Milan, 1997; *In the forbidden city*, Chicago University Press, 2000); and the issue devoted to Italian American women's writings (June 2000).

Sicily is the locale of *La briganta* (Palermo,1990; translated into French as *La briganta*) and *Canto al deserto. Storia di Tina, soldato di mafia* (Milan, 1994). Other works of fiction are: *Complice il dubbio* (Milan, 1992), and *Il paese dei figli perduti* (Milan, 1999). Her most recent publication is a travel journal, *Giorni d'acqua corrente* (Milan, 2002).

Angela M. Jeannet

Born in Pergine Valdarno, AR (1931). Charles A. Dana Professor of Romance Languages, Emerita Franklin and Marshall College, Lancaster, PA 17604-3003 Doctorate in Letters, University of Florence. Diplôme de langue et littérature françaises, University of Lille (France) Her publications include:

New World Journeys-Contemporary Italian Writers and the Experience of America. Ed. and translated with Louise K. Barnett), Greenwood Press, 1977.

Parliamo dell'Italia, University Press of America, 1984.

Natalia Ginzburg: A Voice of the Twentieth Century. Ed. with Giuliana Sanguinetti Katz. University of Toronto Press, 2000.

Under the Radiant Sun and the Crescent Moon. Italo Calvino's Storytelling. University of Toronto Press, 2000. *In forma di corona* (poems). Florence, 2001.

The Edge of Europe by Angela Bianchini. Angela M. Jeannet and David Castronuovo, trs. Afterword by Angela M. Jeannet. University of Nebraska Press, 2000. *Journal* by Maria Bellonci. Mondadori, 2002.

Prof. Jeannet has also published articles on French and Italian twentieth-century fiction and criticism in various collections of essays; also in *Annali d'italianistica, Comparative Literature Studies, Italian Culture, Italica, South Atlantic Review, Stanford Italian Review, Studi novecenteschi*, and *Symposium*.